WHERE ARE YOU NOW?

WHERE ARE YOU NOW?

SARAH CONNELL

The Book Guild Ltd

First published in Great Britain in 2023 by
The Book Guild Ltd
Unit E2 Airfield Business Park,
Harrison Road, Market Harborough,
Leicestershire. LE16 7UL
Tel: 0116 2792299
www.bookguild.co.uk
Email: info@bookguild.co.uk
Twitter: @bookguild

Copyright © 2023 Sarah Connell

The right of Sarah Connell to be identified as the author of this
work has been asserted by them in accordance with the
Copyright, Design and Patents Act 1988.

All rights reserved. No part of this publication may be
reproduced, transmitted, or stored in a retrieval system, in any form or by any means,
without permission in writing from the publisher, nor be otherwise circulated in
any form of binding or cover other than that in which it is published and without
a similar condition being imposed on the subsequent purchaser.

This work is entirely fictitious and bears no resemblance to any persons living or dead.

Typeset in 11pt Minion Pro

Printed and bound in the UK by TJ Books LTD, Padstow, Cornwall

ISBN 978 1915603 487

British Library Cataloguing in Publication Data.
A catalogue record for this book is available from the British Library.

For Paul, Katie and Hannah

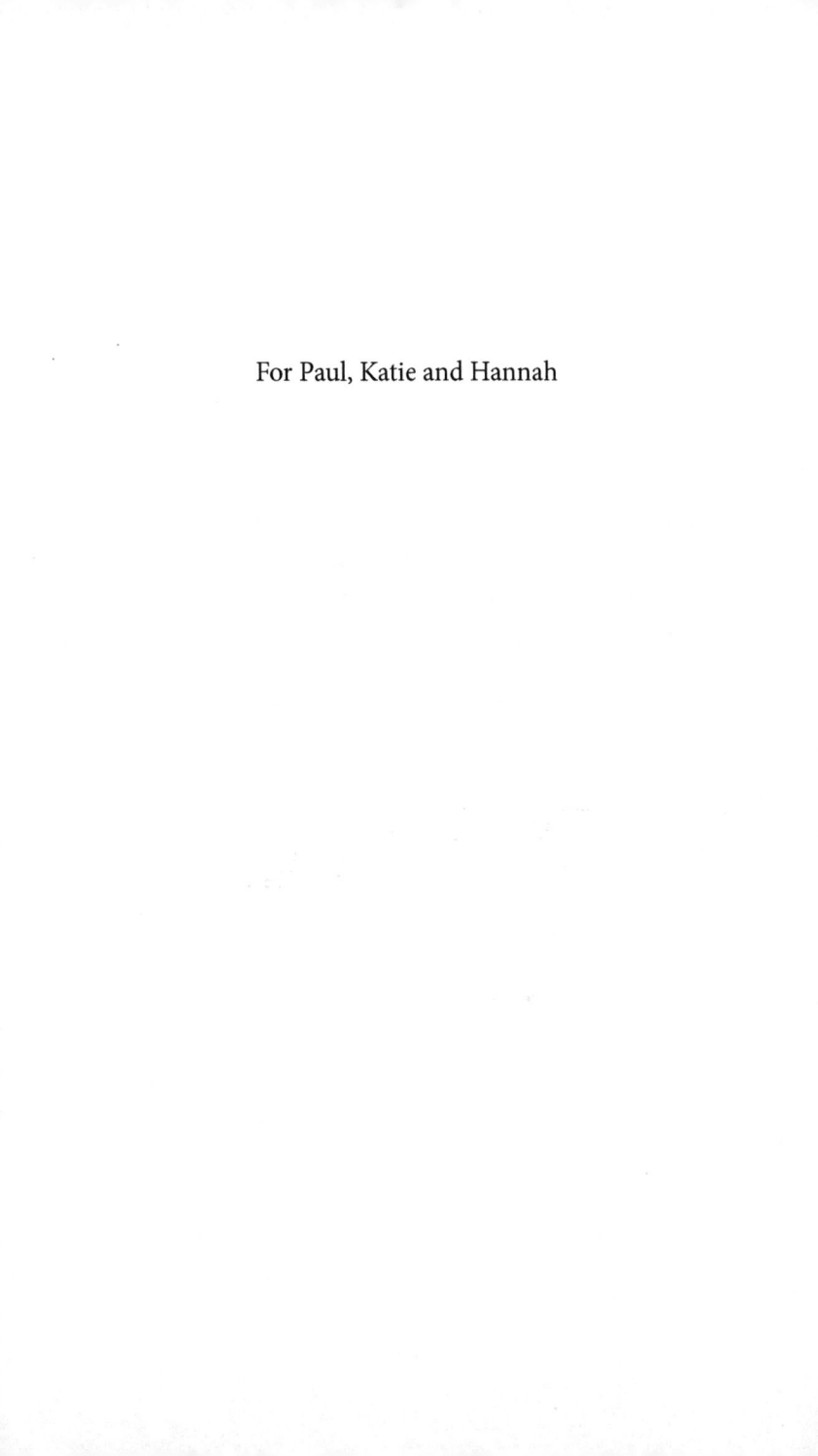

The number of refugees and migrants making the Mediterranean Sea crossing fell in 2018 but it is likely that reductions to search and rescue capacity coupled with an uncoordinated and unpredictable response to disembarkation led to an increased death rate as people continued to flee their countries due to conflict, human rights violations, persecution, and poverty.

UNCHR Dec 2018

The smell of sickness and oldness – it is so disgusting and it's sticking to his skin. His grandfather has been mumbling again; he can't make out the words. Why did his mother expect him to sit here for so long? When is she coming to be the deathbed watcher? The bone claws wave above the sheet. The boy leans forward just enough.

The blue of Walter's eyes has washed away with everything else. He is not frightened now. He wants to know only one thing. Did he do enough? He fixes the boy with the question.

'Was it enough? Could I have done more? Why didn't I do more?'

That is three questions, he knows.

The boy cannot answer, of course. 'Mum is coming. She won't be long.'

'Where is he now?' This is the urgent matter.

'The doctor? Shall I get the doctor?' The boy's voice has risen to a squeak.

The rest of them, his mother, his aunt and Lily should be here. He doesn't know how to help. They have left him alone.

The old man tries to turn in the bed.

'Where is he now?'

PART I

ONE

The fox stopped a few yards away. Its tail frayed, its fur faded, a shabby old man of a fox. It looked directly at him, amber eyes unwavering until it sauntered across the path, picked past the onions lain out to dry and was gone.

Walter let out the breath he had been holding in his chest. Stealthily, as if the fox were watching, he felt into the pocket of his gardening shirt for the little notebook he always shoved in there. The pen was in his back pocket. Flipping the pad open, under the day's entry "Salad crop cleared. Two bolted little gems only good for soup" he wrote "Fox – 7.40am".

In his mind he asked, *Is it you, Mr Reynard, who has been rooting behind my shed, disturbing the pea sticks newly tidied and tied? Could you find anything to eat, any small creatures? You are welcome to any you find. What about windfall apples? There's plenty of them.*

He pushed the pad back in his pocket and went back to his digging. Awake too early again, Walter had come to work off the ache along his limbs with only a hasty cup of tea to sustain him. The list of tasks was long at this time of year. It was satisfying to tick another one off, although his back complained that he had done too much. The soil was heavy from the long drought, difficult to turn; dandelions and chickweed had colonised the patch, unaffected by the lack of rain. The joy was in the sky, minute by minute the darkness giving up its grip, new light seeping over the brambles and the fruit trees. He relished the fresh taste of the air, the turn of the season bringing both fruition and necessary decay. He stood to listen to the blackbird calling from the crab apple tree, more birds joining in with their songs. 'Good morning, all,' he said, his voice loud in the air. No one to hear a foolish old man.

What was that? The figure was a shock, a dark human shape moving out of his sight line. Cautiously, Walter put his fork down, started up the path quietly. There was a man, he was sure of it – it must be an intruder. He had been on his own for an hour or more. It was much too early for any of the other plot holders. Here, only a lonely one who could not sleep. He walked further, acting out as if he was strolling, taking an interest, not focused on the plot ahead. Quietly, swinging his arms, he turned down along Sue's patch, moved slowly back towards the widow's shed.

There was no sign. Whoever it was had gone. Walter walked briskly up the path now, his heart loud in his chest. Towards the back fence, where the new plots had been started, there were fewer obstacles, less cover. But there was no sign of movement. To get out the man must have climbed over the fence, must have run behind the bramble hedges, bent so that his head was unseen. Walter stood, confounded.

There had been no thefts since the council finally fitted a new lock on the main gate after many weeks of gardeners' anger and protest. But now someone was getting in at the back.

He started to go back to his clearing, cleaning for winter, ending summer. But his peace had ended. His back was sore. His stomach made noises. He leant on the fork handle, looking around. The plot at one side was tidy with lack of growth; that gardener had nearly given up, the effort too great for his stiff legs and his need to get to the pub. Glyn with his broad frame would be along soon, eager to escape the cacophony of his home as he relayed it: three adult daughters in full voice and a narrow-faced wife trying to keep control. Glyn's passion was construction, so his plot bloomed wooden frames, an extra shed, piles of bricks assembled just in case.

He was still feeling the startle of seeing someone here who did not belong. The disturbance he noticed behind his shed might not be the fox but this person, glimpsed today. Why was a man coming into these vegetable plots, in this chill early morning? An intruder must be trying to get something, maybe steal something, do damage. It was trespass in any case. So far there had been nothing taken and nothing spoilt. But he knew he should report the sighting to someone. Last year there were some losses. All the widow's Victoria plums lifted at the very moment they were luscious, heavy with ripeness. A couple of people had found tools taken too. Private property did not seem to matter to some. The fox was welcome to his windfalls, but he would be on his guard now if there was a man getting in.

Breakfast was waiting; Walter worked on, digging down for the long stubborn roots of dandelions, pulling up coltsfoot by hand, the earth falling away in dry clumps. The aroma of growth rose from the soil.

If he looked up, not deliberately, casually as if unplanned, he might see her. He has seen her, his wraith, his vision, stretching to pick an apple, bending to regard a daisy. Or she might be pushing the wheelbarrow up the grassy path. Lissom Linda. Lissom is a word he found by chance, a word perfect for his first wife, slender in her early fifties as if still a girl, before she was wrecked by disease and the treatment for the disease, which was worse. She will only come when he is unprepared, not now when he wanted so much to see her. In life she had never been to this vegetable garden of his. *I have changed, Linda, I've had time to change. Look at me. I put stripes on the lawn then because I had to. Look at me now growing things. Come back and see me here.* He knew she would have found delight here; she would have been so pleased with him.

His phone was ringing. It was in a pocket of his jacket left on the bench. It had stopped by the time he had fumbled to pull it out. Gabriella, his stepdaughter. It was barely eight o'clock. Very early for her who rings him infrequently. Hesitating, he held the phone in his palm. It rang again.

'Hi, Gabby. This is an early call. How are you?' He sounded too formal to his own ears.

'Fine, fine, Walter, all fine. Just on my way to work. Someone's got to do it. Haha. Wanted to tell you, I will come down about your birthday next week. Okay.'

She rang off before he could answer. Why does she think she has to come? Marie, her mother, has not said she is coming. Are they going to make a fuss this year especially?

They needn't bother. There's nothing to celebrate in getting older. No word from Celia; the darling daughter had not even mentioned a birthday last time she rang.

The sky had cleared to a misty blue with streaks of early cloud. The beanpoles were still green, but the brown edges of the lower leaves hinted at their ending. He would fill a supermarket bag with runners, a few borlotti, not his favourite but never mind, some kale, curled like sheep's wool and one last courgette – at least he hoped it would be the last. He had embarrassed himself offering courgettes to the neighbours. A polite grimace was all her next door would give him before the stiff refusal: 'We had one last week, Walter, remember.'

'Waste is waste,' he wanted to say. 'This is food, good food.' She was not a cook, not a charmer, his own age but with nothing left of what he could think of as feminine, blocky in the checked trousers and pulled-back hair, her frame too thin. Unbidden, the curves of Sue's outline came to him. She was a new plot holder, younger by twenty years, a small blonde who stirred his interest as she walked up the path waving a greeting, then showing him her back view. He was amused, not guilty, about his wonderings of Sue. He allowed himself one fast image of her in the shed, lying back for him with open arms on the straw bales kept for next year's strawberries. He was smiling as he packed up to go home.

A shape moved out of the side of his eye. Too tall, too high up for the fox. And not his Linda either. A quick flash and it was gone. Was the man still here, moving around, waiting for him to go, perhaps? He stood by the open shed, considering. He put the padlock on the rickety wooden door. The plot holders had the only keys for the gate. He was uneasy, unsure how he should act. He was tired so it was easier to leave it for now; he would see what happened. He had no desire for trouble, for himself or anyone else. He trod through fallen apples, browned, half-eaten by wasps and birds, kicking some aside. Above his head, the branches still held fruit. The shelves in the spare bedroom were filling up.

Eight ounces of self-raising flour, sifted high with one and a half teaspoons of baking powder, two ounces of butter, unsalted of course. Half a pint of liquid, no sour milk today so a little yoghurt added plus one egg beaten. Sugar, just a spoonful and as many sultanas as his hands can carry from the jar. Next week it would be cheese and mustard, a little paprika. He can make six decent-sized ones plus a scruffy mound with the last bits – the oven turned high, ten minutes and his Saturday scones will be on the cooling rack, the smell of warm flour filling the kitchen, each one glossy where he has painted them with the last of the egg. The kettle on, a clean plate, butter in the dish, he can sit and eat at least two with last year's plum jam. The day passes.

This routine, a homage not to Linda but to his second now ex-wife Marie, very much alive, was one he had adopted for afternoons on Saturdays. Routines sweeten time. Sundays are in the pub by twelve so tea and scones are not desirable; by four o'clock he would be asleep, dozing on the sofa.

Four scones sit on a plate, gold and white and brown, soon to be stale, soon to be wasted; he did hate his own weekly waste. He would try again to master half the mixture; so far that experiment had been unsuccessful. Some Saturdays he buttered them, went back to the plot and offered a plateful around to whoever was there. But if he arrived to find only the old boys, he felt a fool. If Sue was there, he could manage a sheepish grin, a "look at me, I have been baking again" demeanour. He wondered now about trying a more ambitious recipe: Chelsea buns to court the lady?

What did he see this day? A fox, an old man, walking his territory, free and unconcerned. No stepdaughters to bother you, Reynard. And someone else, a man's shape half seen among the trees. He would look more carefully from now; there was an intruder, someone who had no right to be there, who was a threat to the peace of the plots and perhaps to their produce. He would keep a watch.

TWO

A circle of grey and white among the scattered colours of fallen leaves on the green. Looking closer, it was fans of feathers, still on the tiny bones, white at the tips, black on the outside. The remains of a feast laid out like chicken bones, chewed and sucked – probably a pigeon, generally despised – perhaps a magpie had met its end here. They were not popular either as they picked off the heads of flowers and new shoots for fun, leaving them littered. One for sorrow, two for joy, birds which childhood had taught him to think of as significant, symbols in a mysterious way. A feast and a death overnight. But certainly not human actions, not the intruder's doing. This morning there was no sign of a man who did not belong.

Glyn was busy building a new structure for his brassicas. He had brought up new planks of wood, his toolbox, and in the wheelbarrow, more compost for his raised beds. Walter looked on, always surprised by the expenditure, *money for soil, mate*, he said to himself, *more money for the dirt you get for free.* His own manure pile, collected from local stables, was satisfyingly high and strong smelling, his plot divided by straight lines, labelled sticks, every section used.

'Heard about the privatisation?' Glyn shouted over.

'How can they privatise us? There's no profit to be made here.'

'Well, it's law now – the council have to put it out to tender, to competition.'

'Who would be interested? Would be a lot of bother and no gain.'

'Someone is, it seems – I heard that there is an eco lot, green something, who are in the running.'

'Who decides?'

'That's the thing; we had those letters, remember? We will be consulted – whatever that is supposed to mean.'

Walter was careful with all official post; his long years in the planning department had left him with efficient habits and a distaste for bureaucratic approaches. Sometimes he thought his working life had been part of an enormous plot called progress which had thrown the old out in favour of the new, the new roads, the new buildings, the new systems. Which then were declared inadequate, unworkable, unnecessary. Or were stopped in their tracks by the next idea or by the tide of paperwork which built sand dunes of opposition.

Now he stacked envelopes unopened on the dining table, reviewed the pile at intervals, then threw away those with addresses on the back he considered unnecessary. Digital messages were equally unimportant to him. He was easily bored by his forays into the internet and frustrated by his lack of speed and skill in navigation.

'We'll find out soon enough.' Walter shook his head and shook off the problem. While he dug up the courgette plant, consigning it still green and fertile to the compost, Glyn's hammering sounded loudly in the clear air.

'And have you heard about the fruit theft?'

'Fruit? What fruit?'

'That new girl, Sue, her store of pears has all been pinched, taken overnight.'

A group of plot holders were gathering up the path near Sue's patch. The couple who divided the work on strict gender lines, the young man who only came every third week and used a strimmer with enthusiasm, the woman who grew flowers in rows and her husband who dug everything up, the widow who had built a pergola to sit under and drink, the Polish lady who grew nettles for soup, Harry who used chemical fertilisers and grew the largest of everything. Walter joined them, standing at the back, listening. The voices were rising with anxiety and a hint of anger into the morning cool.

The new secretary for the Beetham Road Allotments was a young woman, Frederica, known as Freddie. She was in the centre of a swirl of complaints and questions.

'That shed was just too easy to break into. She needs a good padlock.'

'Why was she keeping them all in there?'

'No room at home. We haven't all got cellars. The shed should be a safe place.'

'Nar. If they are serious, they will get in. The council have got to protect us.'

'We had thefts last year – all those plums went overnight off my tree. Those pears will end up on a market stall.'

'That's organised – they need stuff to carry them in.'

'Somebody has got to do something.'

'What can we do to get the council to listen?'

'It's not safe for any of us, if people can just walk in.'

Harry, round and broad, always in shorts whatever the season, his thick legs lumpy and veined, spoke up as if to summarise.

'It's illegal and we must get it stopped.' Heads nodded.

Walter shuffled forwards a little between the shoulders and said, 'I have seen someone, not sure exactly, but there was a man, I think a man.'

Now the voices grew shrill, and everyone turned to look at him, to bombard him with queries. Faces grew tense and nasty. He was uncertain of what else to say; all he had seen was a human outline, and the disturbance behind his shed. He raised his hands, shrugged. 'It was a man's shape, a thin man I would say.'

'Can you get the council officer down here again, Freddie?'

He was grateful that the attention turned to Frederica. An unusual name, perhaps she had Danish or Swedish origins. Piercings, a cloud of red hair, four children, one at the breast, she was a Viking queen, a warrior. Strong legs and leaking breasts, a compact rear – Walter could trust her to find out the fruit robbers, it must be more than one, and bring them to justice. He was a little afraid of her as she patrolled up and down the central path with a child in tow, looking and commenting. She was an eco-type, no slug pellets on her task list. Walter kept his killer sprays out of sight at the back of the shed, hidden by the wheelbarrow. There was no official ruling about being organic. His manure pile was proudly visible to all. Protection for his crops, that was another matter.

She tried to move away, stepping slowly, back to her plot, reassuring as she went that she would ring the council in the week. Some voices continued to chew over the facts; the story began to be decorated with warnings of further invasion, of a professional gang of thieves at large.

Walter walked away; he said nothing more to contribute to the discussion. He heard the complaining continuing behind him. People were entitled to be cross and to be worried, but he didn't like the tone. Some people liked a chance to cast blame, to be nasty. It could go too far. The shape of the man he had glimpsed was of someone thin, almost slender, no sign of boxes or bags for the fruit, just a swift-footed visitor. He was uncomfortable, but for no reason he could understand, he wished now he had not said anything. So far, he had no evidence of actual harm; even the mess behind the shed could have been the fox rooting for grubs. Those pears of Sue's, an early French variety, her harvest, gone in her first year. He would be furious himself at the loss. How dare strangers take what had cost so much effort and care. But that outline did not suggest an efficient thief. His apples would not be ready for a week or two; The Bramley tree was dropping windfalls now, but that fruit would not be properly ripe until late October.

In his notebook, he recorded the sighting of a man. He decided, if he saw him again, he would definitely report it properly. Or he would try to catch the intruder himself and warn him off. That would be the best course of action, the least fuss and trouble that way. Walter avoided trouble in his life. As he walked home, he debated trying to speak to Celia. He would ring her and see if she answered. Sometimes she did. Sometimes he would get a message later saying she was busy, promising to ring when she could. His only daughter, the lovely girl. He could not expect to have her attention very often. It was Gabriella who made a point of calling him.

When it became clear that Linda's diagnosis was serious, Celia was in the last year of her degree in Manchester. He thought she would take time off, ask the university to give her compassionate leave from her studies. He struggled to find the words to tell his daughter that Linda might be gone in a matter of months, maybe less. At the last, the doctors offered a new treatment; innovation, could extend life, a few months, maybe longer, the empty words that came to mean research with more suffering. Walter expected his daughter to be there. He needed her with him now. Surely her mother must need her only child. Linda chided him, consoled him that the degree was too important, Celia would come when she could. A few times in those terrible days, she did arrive to sit with her mother for one night at a time, relieving him so he could do a day's work – his department had been very understanding.

The agony of her death, when it came, was his alone. He was glad then as he carried her upstairs in his arms on the final evening, as Linda screamed at him to stop hurting her, why was it happening, what had she done to deserve it, glad that their daughter could not hear it, the bitterness and pain that wracked her mother's frame at the end. He bent over that bed, unable to speak or cry, relieved that it was over and sick with the knowledge of that relief.

Celia came home the next day, shook in his arms with dry sobs while he tried to tell her something of the truth. He expected her to be close, to stay with him afterwards, not to leave him alone. She went straight back to her shared house after the funeral, rang him once a week dutifully. When she graduated and started legal training, it became clear she would stay in that city. Now she has a job and her own flat. His dear daughter has become cool and distant as if her mother had been the link between them. He does not know if she is happy, who her friends are. He is her duty visit, her duty call, the cuddles of the past lost as if they had never been. Often, he rehearses conversations with her, imaginary moments when he tells her how Linda sometimes haunts him, a wraith, a longed-for vision out of reach.

Supper would be soup. The beetroots, muddy globes larger than last year as it seems they liked the lack of rain, will need to be scrubbed first, then boiled for ten minutes, just enough to make them easier to skin, rubber gloves on. They give off a smell of the earth they have been lifted from. Then an onion, a fat one of his own, softened in butter, a potato or two skins on, chopped and added – the crop was poor this year because of the drought but there was still a harvest – then the beets, vegetable stock from powder, simmered an hour or so. Then carefully blended to make a bright pink soup, splashes all over to be cleaned up. A big bowlful with yoghurt plopped in and hot toast, going straight into the bloodstream.

THREE

There in the soft earth by the leaf mould heaps, a footprint. A clear shoe print. It could be his own, but scrutinised, it was smaller. Had the shape and outline of a trainer. He never wore trainers to the allotments himself. Could be anyone of the other plot holders, having a walk around looking at the other gardens as he often did himself. But it could be the trespasser, the intruder he had seen. Someone, who did not belong, was coming in here. Someone who had no right to be on this ground. A thief or worse.

Behind the shed, there were signs of someone moving the bean sticks which were carefully tied together in a long bundle; the weed buckets had been upended, and his pile of potting tubs moved to one side. The shed was an organised, clean space with hooks for the main tools and shelves for the netting and a variety of useful objects. He was careful to keep things behind it in order too. Periodically, he sorted and stacked those odds and ends which did not fit inside or for which he had not found a place yet. Now he could see clear signs of someone else's hands, not his own.

At home, the dinner would be ready; the comforting aroma of stew would be filling the kitchen. Cubes of shin beef, carefully browned first in butter with a splash of oil, then put aside, onions and carrots, pieces of parsnip and some swede too, all sweated in butter until the aroma rises, put the beef back in, add a glass of red wine if it's there, then hot water, a stock cube, a bouquet garni of bay leaf, thyme and rosemary tied up with string, or a sachet of dried herbs in the winter, and into a very low oven to simmer for at least four hours. Mushrooms are sometimes waiting to be softened and added near the end, also an inevitable courgette. He put a pan of peeled potatoes ready for boiling and mashing.

On Sundays Walter cooked first so that when he walked in after his pub afternoon, the aroma of casserole greeted him. If he was unorganised, or feeling too down to bother, then it would have to be a pizza from the freezer, and those were bad days. When he lived with women, his lovely Linda and then the energetic and exhausting Marie, Walter had not cooked. The emptiness of life without work, and without a companion in his house, his bed, his kitchen, had to be filled. He liked to eat, and now he had learnt that he liked to cook. Slowly, with an open cookbook propped on the counter, with much swearing and more splash, he had conquered the meals he remembered. He had branched out into wilder realms over time, as he longed for those sharp, sweet flavours which came in a takeaway.

On the way back today, he had had the thought to call in at the allotment. Dinner was waiting; he had time to check; he was not sure if anything needed checking, but the idea of a trespasser would not go away. It was his habit to stay away from gardening on Sundays, to let beer and relaxation swallow up the hours. A back-of-the-mind thought about the thefts, the disturbance at the shed, the man he thought he had seen; he would just take a quick look. He could call it a patrol. The key was in his trousers as if he had planned this.

Now here were signs of someone, of something out of order, at the least a troubling disturbance and maybe more. Walter was not inclined to panic. Carefully, he picked his way over the damp grass, keeping his shoes as clean as possible – he would take them off as soon as he was indoors and clean them off. He pulled on the padlock to the shed to make sure it was firm. You would need serious equipment to break it. But someone was using this space.

He had set off for the pub to walk the route he always used: down his street of thirties semis, along past the tall Victorian houses stretching up above the bend in the road, past the turning for the allotments, then along past the private school fields. He could go a number of ways in this small city to reach his Sunday pub. He chose the shortest every time, cutting through the college grounds, skirting the recently new town hall, where it stands as a modern mirror to the imposing façade of County Hall, built when the city commanded the centre of the region. Once he reached the road which heads west out of town, he crossed, past the car park and into the huddle of low buildings which includes his favourite place, where he can meet his oldest friends.

'Hey up.' A greeting from Bernie, standing at the bar as usual. This old colleague had taken to retirement as a pastime and was here most days.

'How you doing? On a health kick yet? You are letting

that grow a bit much, aren't you?' Walter pointed gently at the swelling stomach.

Bernie raised his glass. 'Don't be a bore, Swivel Hips.' This caused a ripple around the bar and brought a grin to Walter's face.

'In any case, as I've told you, they don't put bay windows in a slum.' The line was not a new one, but Bernie always delivered it with a self-satisfied flourish. Walter joined the laughter. He was secretly proud of his own appearance. In the mirror what he sees is not bad, my boy. The jacket is an old friend, the corduroy collar a little faded, the suede worn in what you could call an interesting way. The blue button-down shirt is freshly ironed. Hair is still thick; brushed back it almost looks as it once did. Grey is a distinguished colour in a man. Gabby had made him smile saying that.

He looked around at those who were drinking every Sunday afternoon, in this old-style bar, no music and only one machine, most importantly, proper beer, a selection of brews and of breweries to be discussed and sampled. The walls still retain the staining of decades of cigarette smoke and the stale remembrance lingers on a warm day. The usual suspects are all here, the faces he has seen all his life: a neighbour from his street, a bloke he went to school with, there a man he has worked with, over by the fruit machine that strange individual who owned the old record shop, now sadly closed. Many of these regulars come in weekday evenings too; they are middle aged or older, with just a couple of younger ones, very few women, although Walter knew their faces and remembered their names too.

Not many younger drinkers, it is too early in the day.

Later they might be out again, doing the "run", as many drinking holes as possible before raiding the kebab shops. They might come in here for one drink, but they favoured the huge spaces filled with loud music and cheap lagers.

Once, the nightclubs in the town had been famous all over the north, coaches bringing them from other bigger cities. The streets were full of half-naked partygoers until dawn and the police went in pairs. It was quieter now – no one had the money; the drink was cheaper by far in the shops; the spirit of wild fun had been lost along with the factories and the mines.

'Howdy.' Frank's greeting was a formula, said with a nod and glass in hand.

Walter had known Frank since primary school, although friendship did not flourish until they were teenagers, both on scooters, matching their clothes to the idols of the time, learning the tunes of rebellious songs to practise badly on guitars. Once Frank had curly hair down to his shoulders and had even come home from university with a velvet jacket and a temporary obsession with Oscar Wilde. Now he had the appearance of a monk, his tonsure polished, his face long and grave. He has the habit of touching his face, palm up, rubbing around his brow and nose. He repeats the movement regularly. Walter had never noticed it until the time Celia persuaded him for once to let her sit with his "drinking friends", saw him in action and complained of it all the walk home. Now he often thought, when the third pint was slipping down, that he could time it by the pub clock behind Frank's head.

There is a web of connections, many old and frayed,

links to places and times past. The streets of the town are layered with his memories, shadows of happenings, feelings, flashes of what has gone and what remains. Apart from that short period of escape to university in the big city, Walter has lived in this place all his life. The city has changed around him, losses and progress marking the years together in raw-looking brick, concrete and the bright colours of new buildings in square blocks.

Walter joined Frank at the table, which was recognised as theirs, him and Frank, with Gerry the ex-miner, who now arrived.

Frank had been a distribution manager for the biggest catalogue firm, in the days when a glossy home catalogue was a joy for children's hopes and a resource for everyone's shopping. He achieved early retirement just as the need for those tomes was disappearing with the option of screens and instant satisfaction. He spent his time now on the internet.

'Have you been watching those pictures from Gaza?' A peaceful perusal of the beer and chat about the latest TV drama was put aside. 'Those young kids throwing stones? Up against soldiers in riot gear. Terrible, isn't it? Getting worse too. Terrible waste of life. Imagine if you were born a Palestinian, eh?'

Walter thought of what he had seen, the dust obscuring faces, the chaos, people in danger and pain. He looked down into his glass as if to find a solution there.

Gerry shook his head in a gesture of complacent agreement. Walter wondered if he could find anything to say, if there was anything to say, anything to do. How distant their shock and anger was, the response of those unaffected in any real way. He knew he was leading a quiet life by choice, a life on the edge of the world, away from action.

'We don't know how lucky we are. How safe,' he said.

'That's one thing we've got,' Frank agreed. 'Haha, born English is our only advantage, and that's slipping away with this government. Did you see that article? Did you read that plonker on Brexit? Don't people see the figures, can't they add it up?' Frank loved to analyse the current political crisis at home. He was someone who knew the polling figures, remembered previous election results to the last bit of relevant data. But like Walter, he no longer had faith in solutions.

'What about that bus then? They can tell lies; we all know it's a lie – extra money for the NHS, they don't want the NHS, want to run it down. Get their greedy hands on the profit. Why doesn't the right-wing media say so? They're all in on it. All got their fingers in the pie.'

Gerry had a core of bitterness like all those who had held the faith during the national miners' strike. Politics was an urgent subject for him. He would not join discussions about music, kept quiet if they strayed into something he thought of as academic, his graduate friends showing the education which he was always conscious he lacked. The running club had brought him into this circle, in the days when Frank ran every Saturday afternoon and Walter continued to refuse to come along. Squash club had been his thing.

'We need a revolution in this country, that's what we need. You can't deny it when we've got this lot in power. Just look at the history, will you. See what they really want to do with us.'

Gerry needed to sound off about the government at intervals and they were his audience. His wife had left him during the strike after joining the women's groups which flourished in its wake, and he only saw his grown-up children occasionally. These friends shared his views, but they lacked his conviction that their opinions mattered.

Bernie heard the words Gerry was using and came over to join in. 'So, once we're out of Europe, will all these Polish delis we've got now, will they have to close then? Will they all have to clear off?'

A general shrug. Who knows?

'If you go in for a look, you've got no idea what's there as all the labels are in Polski. What use is that? And they won't tell you; they don't want you in there, won't speak English.'

Walter wanted to make a defence. 'I like one of the sausages from the deli near the bus station. It is just spicy enough, good in a sandwich. They cut a few slices, nice and thin, as few as you want.'

'We're not going out of Europe,' Frank asserted. 'No one can think that's a good idea. Do you want to be stopped from all your trips to Spain, Bernie? You'd need a visa, and let's face it, they won't let you in.'

General laughter. But also some grumbling noises from men standing at the bar. The topic has become a tricky one for public discussion. This pub is too small a space; there is not enough room for real difference. Frank and Walter exchange rueful glances.

'People round here should wake up.' Walter lowered his voice carefully and said in all seriousness, 'Look at how much money came in from Europe after the mines closed.'

Unimpressed, shaking his head, Bernie went back to his stand at the bar.

Walter's grandfather had been a miner. It was a matter of family pride that his father, and then he, had escaped that route and had jobs where you and your lungs stayed clean all day. The pit where Grandad had worked was now a museum, where people could pay to go down into the depths and the darkness, trying, if they might, to imagine the noise, the heat and filthy dust, the bare bodies bent double. But in the villages where there had been black money earnt the hard way, now sons and grandsons had no route ahead, no path to swerve from. Whole communities were broken now.

Gerry entertained his friends with a satirical account of the parliamentary processes of the week, making them laugh and prompting Frank to repeat a quote from an article he had read. It was Walter's turn to order another round.

Now back on his plot, all was still; no one else was about as the afternoon drew down to chilly dusk. But there was a footprint and there were signs of an intruder. Ready for home and food, unsure of his motives, he went up the path to where he had the apple trees.

The Newton Wonders were not ready, needed another two or three weeks to fall into your hand, red and yellow monster apples, sharp and sweet together. Not his favourite ones as they did not cook well, but as Frankie had praised him, a "heritage" variety. Perhaps the pear robbers had tasted one and decided against picking his crop. He gave one and then another a quick tug and took them back down to the bench. He put the two apples there, in the middle, clear to see. Let's find out if you are here. He smiled as he turned for home. This is not the Garden of Eden, but it is my patch of heaven. Steal my apples. Come and get them.

Later he would ponder on how he had done such a simple thing, something he had not planned to do and could not explain but an action which led to such a different way ahead.

As soon as he opened the door of the house, the smell of food filled the hall and the kitchen with a welcome invitation to a tray by the fire. If there was only nonsense and crime on the TV, he was sure to find a chef cooking for the camera in a huge glossy kitchen, comfort watching.

FOUR

The apples had gone. Vanished completely. He searched for a half-eaten remain, which a large bird might have made of one, or perhaps the fox if it was really hungry. But they had been taken.

The morning was foggy; the air made his ears tingle. It would soon be time for a hat. Slowly, with care, he searched the plot: checked the spinach, the last beetroots, the line of kale and leeks planted together, the parsnips showing long, green tops. He walked up to the apple trees. He had picked the Pippins last week and the plums and damsons were stewed and jammed last month. The Newton Wonders were heavy on the boughs. He must pick them soon. There was no sign of anything having been taken; nothing was missing. Only the two apples he had set out as an offering or a trap, he was not sure which.

Later a fuss started. Old Harry, who was round and loud, shouted to everyone who would stop to listen that he was sure someone had been into his shed. As this rickety construction was certainly not secure, the crowd who had gathered generally agreed that he was lucky his tools had not gone.

'Why get into a shed if not to steal? Sue had all her pears stolen.' Harry had no answer to his own question. 'What about that man you saw, Walter?'

Walter thought of the apples, but he shook his head as if he had nothing to say. Harry looked as if he would question him, but after a few seconds, he turned and walked away. The crowd dispersed muttering about trespassers and the need for security. Voices were still raised as Glyn joined Walter to walk back down the path.

'Sue's put a padlock on now, but if thieves are determined that won't stop them. It's not that hard to break a padlock if you've got the equipment,' he said quietly. 'You haven't seen anyone again then?'

Walter felt he did not know enough; he could not say who had taken his apples, or if this meant the intruder was a thief lurking on the plots. No tools had been stolen from old Harry's shed, so no harm done so far. He had no wish to let people start a hunt; he did not want anyone attacked. He had a clue, but it was his, and he would keep it to himself, for now at least.

His plan for the day had included moving some of the fruit bushes, to give the redcurrant space. So now he must return to it. He was glad of the cool and the first damp layer of earth waiting for him and his fork. Now as the year turned into October, the rains had arrived, but they only wetted the surface of the soil. It was still hard work to turn it. He went back to his digging, working the soil to a softness that the fruit bushes could bed into as their new home. His back hurt by the time he had made progress, but where he was working, the earth had changed. He took a handful and let it fall, a rich crumb.

The summer, the continual heat, had flattened the landscape, subtracted the green. On their summer walking day this year, he and his friends had found the Dales transformed; the grey stones divided squares of russet and gold, rather than green; trees drooped over the trickle of the river. It was easy to hop and stride over the flat boulders to reach the centre where the brown water flowed narrowly, shallow enough to spot minnows and even trout in places.

Although they had started early, it was soon too hot for a brisk pace. They ate pork pies for lunch, grateful for the shade of the river path. Frank wore a wide-brimmed hat tied firmly under his chin and repeatedly mopped his face.

'This is it, then. Global warming,' he said.

'Yorkshire warming anyway,' Gerry replied mournfully.

'Don't remember it this hot for years.'

'Short memories then,' Walter insisted. 'It reached over thirty degrees two years ago. It's just that it was cool last summer. Mind you it was hot in spring, that's true.' He recorded temperatures at key moments in the year in his notebook so he was certain of his facts, a comfortable position he liked to be in.

This autumn day, once his planned work was done, he picked four of the red and yellow speckled apples from his tree before he went home. He put them all on the bench, in clear view.

In the kitchen he fried a small piece of white fish, bathing it in warm olive oil with parsley, capers and garlic. Afterwards, there was the last of the apple pie, crumbly pastry mixed with an egg and windfalls from the Bramley tree sweetened to a perfect sharpness.

FIVE

He had a clear view, at the back of Sue's plot. The shape of a man was visible by her shed as he went up to look at the apple trees again. It was drawing into evening, earlier every day now, so he was ready to stretch out and go home. No one else was left. Now he saw the intruder was here.

He liked to walk about the whole space on his own in the quiet, looking over the patches of cultivation, some organised, many half-tended, on their way to being lost to weeds and grass. People did not have the time, busy with work and families, did not realise that it was not like the gleaming photos in books or on the TV; growth came hard, the labour unremitting, they had not understood the necessity to inhabit their plots, to learn them, to feel the soil and weather, to know the land. As daylight ended, Walter felt the earth freeing itself from the hoe and the spade. He imagined the natural life here, separate from the humans; this was the territory of the fox and the birds, the bees and the unseen crawling creatures. Wildness was always at the edges, waiting.

Lifting his head to watch a roosting line of pigeons across the dusky sky, he had spotted him. This time Walter was quick enough. There he was, a man, bent over the water butt, splashing his face.

'Who are you? What are you doing here? You know you are trespassing. What is your name?'

Walter looked at him, astonished at the reality; there was an intruder, a foreign invader. A young man, dark hair, a face that struck you as handsome but hollow, with large brown eyes meeting Walter's own, a soft mouth. He was wearing a smart jacket, the kind young men favoured, not warm enough for the chill of the evening. On his feet he wore trainers, with the colours of a fashionable make.

'Osama.'

Walter stared.

'That is my name: Osama.' The man did not seem to be frightened or intimidated.

'Are you eating my apples?' The question sounded ridiculous.

'Thank you, sir. Yes, I am very grateful.'

His voice was low, harmonious, his English clear but accented.

'Did you take a lot of pears from one of the sheds?'

'No, sir.' This with a lift of his head, almost defiance or perhaps pride.

'Where are you from?'

'Palestine.'

Walter thought of the television scenes and the conversation in the pub. This was someone from there, who had lived there, seen the uprising, been one of those in that faraway place. He was confused, uncertain what to say or do. Osama, a strange sound for a name; it had an echo to it which he could not place.

'I'm sorry. But you can't stay here. This is, it's other people's property. People will be angry if they catch you.' He thought as he said it, that this was a kind of lie. He was angry himself.

The man looked away over the plots and was silent.

'You have no right to be here. You must know that you are on other people's land.'

'Oh yes, sir. I know that.'

'That won't do, no lad, that won't do.' Walter found he had nothing more to say. He stood there on the path. He looked at the man's profile. The darkening air was making his ears sting. He had better ring the police. Or perhaps he would tell Freddie on his way home, let her handle it. He must report the intruder to someone. After a few seconds, he turned to walk away, thoughtful and uncertain, planning how to act.

As he neared his own plot, he looked back and saw the man was climbing over the broken piece of fence at the rear of the site. In a moment, while Walter watched, he was gone.

Perhaps there was no need to say anything to anyone. No harm was done, so far at least. Perhaps he would wait and see.

As he left for home, he was surprised to see a new notice pinned to the frame of the main gate: "Please will all plot holders come to a meeting at six on Friday by the gate".

Frederica must have put it up earlier while he was too busy to see.

Walter walked back to his warm house, to a supper

of pasta with homemade tomato sauce, an onion, garlic, sweated down, then chopped tomatoes and basil added, a pinch of chilli flakes, slow cooked till thick and seasoned, then grated cheese, not parmesan today but never mind, and a big green salad.

As he pulled back the duvet that night, he paused. A full harvest moon hung in the night sky, filling the window with moonlight, laying brightness as a blanket over the lawn outside and over his own empty bed. He stood at the window for a minute or two, gazing out at the brilliance. He looked for Linda, as if she might be passing there, a vision to console him. He wondered what she would say about the young man, what she would tell him to do.

*

The next day he went early, intent on seeing if there were any traces of the invasion. He walked along the paths between plots, searching for signs. Just by the widow's shed, Osama appeared, startling him so that he stopped abruptly. His heart began to speed.

'You're still here.' His voice was shrill to his own ears.

'I have nowhere to go. I slept at my friend's before, but now I have nowhere.'

'Okay,' Walter said. He felt how inadequate this was. He felt he was not able to act, to say the useful thing, to be strong.

'But this is no place for you. I will have to report you. You are trespassing. You know what that means?'

'Please do not do that.' The young man looked directly at Walter.

He was polite, calm, his face had a charming quality which caught your attention.

'If you report me, they will detain me. They will lock me up. They will deport me.'

Detain. Deport. Ugly words.

'Deport you? So you do have no right to be here at all.'

The man shrugged; hopelessness seemed to flow down his body as if it was a hollow vessel.

'Isn't there somewhere else for you, a shelter for the homeless, a charity?' Walter's words sounded foolish to himself.

'There is nowhere for people like me.'

He did not look like the people sleeping in doorways so often now on the streets of the town. He did not look wrecked. He was composed again, meeting Walter's eyes. He looked thin, but healthy, attractive. He was a surprising type of invader. Walter was unsure what he should be doing. The man was what everyone called an illegal. He was on other people's land and all those people would be sure he was a thief.

There seemed no questions to cover what he would like to know, what he was ignorant of. For no reason he could have identified to anyone, he felt ashamed.

'You'll have to be careful. People won't like it.'

He walked away, without saying anything more. As he reached the main path, he turned back to look. The young man was standing where he had left him, his eyes following. For a second, they held each other's gaze.

'Help yourself to apples from the tree,' he called out. He could hear the man's thank yous repeated as he cleared up his tools and locked the shed. All the time he felt the presence of the figure behind him, somewhere on the plot. He did not try to look again, but he knew there was a young man standing, walking, hiding, a person who did not belong, should not be here, was trespassing. A person who had nowhere to go except this patch of other people's vegetable gardens in the late autumn cool.

SIX

Got you. There you are. He had caught him. It felt like catching, like a kind of hunt in the dark of evening, as Osama was careful, necessarily secretive, able to blend in behind the brown debris of winter. Walter had found a rolled-up blanket, wrapped in sheets of cardboard. It was tucked close to the fence behind one of the many blackberry thickets, only visible if you were looking for it very carefully.

It had started with the apples. One Saturday he left his spare scones, three of them buttered and wrapped in greaseproof. When he went down to see in the gloom of the next October dawn, there was no sign of the package. A week later when he had made a quantity of root vegetable soup, he put some in an old mug, hot when he left the house, covered in foil, prominently placed on the bench. He thought he would have liked to leave a note, with details of the vegetables he had used, a wish that it could be eaten still warm. But could this young man read English? He apparently spoke it well enough from their brief encounters, but reading and understanding the alphabet – that might be different. In any case, what was he doing, thinking of notes for a stranger who is trespassing? What was he doing, secretly cooking for this stranger?

Walter was determined to speak to him again. This day he left after putting food on the bench, locked the gate, walked home, turned round and came back. Very quietly he lifted the padlock on the gate, crept in as if he had no right to enter and there the true intruder was, on the bench, unfolding the silver paper to reveal the package of food.

'Don't get up, it's okay, stay there; I only want to talk to you. Eat first.'

Osama stopped, holding the piece of quiche awkwardly in the air, as Walter approached.

'No, please, talk first, sir. I can eat this later.' He put the food carefully down on the foil it had been wrapped in.

'Well, if you like. How are you?' This question sounded cheap and ridiculous to him. 'Tell me about your situation. I am not going to do you any harm, I promise.'

'I am an asylum seeker. I came here for that.'

'I see. When was that?'

'Five years ago. But I have been refused.'

'Why is that?'

'Perhaps because I am Palestinian.'

'Surely not. That would be a reason to offer you—'

'My papers are not good enough, they say. Palestine does not have an embassy here in the UK. So it is hard to get support.'

This information fitted with the brief research Walter had already done. Despite his resistance to internet searches, now motivated by an idea he could not release himself from, he had been on several websites and knew that if people's papers were not up to date or inconsistent in some way, the Home Office might refuse asylum whatever their circumstances. He had made a note of some facts about this, numbers and countries involved. His garden notebook had a dual purpose now.

Osama and Walter sat silently for a few moments.

'You are from Gaza?'

Osama's eyes flickered and then he nodded.

'I am refused. So I cannot work. I cannot claim your benefit. I am no one.'

He spread his hands in front. 'Yet you see me. Here I am.'

'You said you could be detained?'

'Yes, sir, I was detained. Once. They charge you, stand over you like thugs in uniform. Into a van and into detention with you. Off the streets, into a cell. They say it is not a cell. But it is.'

Walter nodded as if he understood, although he knew he did not.

'They keep the light on, you know? All day, all night a bright blue light. In your cell for twenty days they held me like that.' Walter made an attempt at a nod.

'The second time I ran away.'

Walter stared. 'You ran away from detention?'

'From the men, the officers. I could not go back. I will not go back.'

Walter felt bewilderment swamp him. He had drawn close to something terrible.

'I was living with an Iranian then. He was okay, but he liked me to cook for him and his friends, a kind of rent you might say. So I was in the kitchen chopping vegetables. The doorbell rings.'

Walter watched the man's hands exploring the story as he talked.

'Six police officers. Yes, six of them, all wearing the jackets, the bombproof ones. Big men, all together, pushing into the flat. One has the cuffs holding out ready for me.'

'Why do they send six?'

Osama shrugged. 'Who knows what they do or why they do it. Maybe they think I am dangerous. Me, a bad man? I don't know. I am in my vest, house shoes. They are like an army. Do you know that, sir?'

'No, I did not know that.'

'One holds out the cuffs. I am supposed to put out my arms and go. Go there, wait for how long, how many months, how many years maybe. I know what is like in there. People stay for years, you know. And not knowing.' He lowered his head, grasping the back of his neck as he gazed down at the path. 'You do not know when or why.'

Walter had tried to find out the specifics about detention centres, had researched the stories online. Still, that had been on-screen. This man was telling him something he had experienced.

Osama stood now in front of him, looked directly at him.

'So I said to him, the one with the handcuffs, if you try to put those on me I will slit my throat, like this.' He gestured with a sharp slice of his hand. For a second, the long blade of a knife flashed in Walter's face.

'What on earth happened?'

'They all stand back. A circle of them. Standing there.

They did not move. I had the knife in my hand. Holding only, no threat. I saw the door was open, the hall was empty. I dropped the knife and I ran. I ran and I ran. They did not follow me. I don't know why.' He laughed a grim short bark. 'I ran down the stairs, out of the door, into the street. I ran and I ran. I could not go to one of those terrible places again.'

Walter felt as if a hole had opened in the ground or the sky. He had no idea how to respond. His research had not prepared him for this. The man was so angry. The tale so terrible.

'You get lost there. Forgotten. Thrown away.' Osama's eyes challenged Walter, a fierce stare he could not meet. He looked away at the plot as if to find an answer there.

Walter could hear their breathing in the evening air. Then Osama lifted his head. 'No torture at least. Not like my country.'

Walter focused his eyes on the pastry, crumbling onto the foil wrapping beside them.

Needing a change of gear, he asked, 'Do you eat meat?' The question seemed absurd and yet was a relief.

'I do eat meat. But I am Muslim.'

'Muslim, yes, of course, I thought that would be it. So only halal meat then?'

'Yes, sir.'

'Don't call me, sir. My name is Walter.'

'Walter.'

'How do you spell your name?'

Osama responded with his direct gaze. Walter felt now like an interrogator, but also that he had a right to know more than he did. Osama slowly spelt out the strange list of letters.

Emboldened, Walter asked, 'What happened to you?'

'What do you want to know, Walter?'

'Well, why you came here?' Osama shook his head. He had tightly curled hair, cut short. A beard was growing on his lower chin. Walter felt this question was wrong. 'Sorry, you don't have to tell me anything. But do tell me how you came to be sleeping here.'

'My friend, I sleep on his floor for a long time, but the landlord came, he say no subtenant – is that the word? – and my friend, he is happy because he is, I don't know how to say it, but he wants me to go.'

'How do you manage, in the daytime I mean?'

There was no answer, only a quiet smile and a shrug which was enough for Walter to realise he had gone too far.

'I must go, Osama. I will leave you something tomorrow.'

'You are very good. You are like my father.' He was polite and something more; Walter thought his tone warm and pleasing.

'You speak good English. You have had an education. You went to school, you studied English?'

'Yes, English is very important. I like it.' This did not answer Walter's question. He hesitated to push for more. He felt it was a pleasure to speak to Osama without understanding his own response. He must accept what he was told. There was no harm in this man, no wrong in his small use of the property of others. Walter had told no one and now he was sure he would tell no one. He would not risk anyone else knowing, would not bring risk to this man. He had a secret which he would hold close.

About to walk away, he hesitated.

'Is your father alive?'

'Yes, but he is very old.'

Old as me, very old, he thought to himself ruefully. He stopped at the gate, padlock in his hand, and called out, 'Can I bring you something else?' Osama shook his head, crumbs falling from his lips.

I will bring him a warmer jacket, Walter decided as he went home.

SEVEN

Freddie, her long red-gold hair hidden by a thick woollen cap, had brought flasks of scented herbal tea, cups and a big tin of lumpy flapjacks designed to break teeth. The plot holders gathered eagerly around her offerings, each sure that they would not stay more than a few minutes on this chilled, murky evening. There was enough light from the street lamp at this end near the gate, but many had torches.

'Okay, folks, I have an agenda. Please be patient, I am not used to this role, meetings like this.' A sandy-haired child tugged at her jacket and she turned to look down and talk to him.

'Well, we know what the most important thing is, don't we?' It was Harry, round and loud.

Mutterings swelled in agreement.

'There is someone living on the allotments. A homeless junkie or one of those illegals.'

'I don't think that's true. Have you actually seen anything?' Freddie asked.

'I'm sure there's someone.' Harry raised his voice to a shout. 'I've seen someone moving about. We all have, haven't we?'

There were shrugs, but no one replied. In fact, had anyone seen Osama? Walter looked around the circle of faces; they were all there, the serious ones and the newbies who still thought it was an easy hobby. The horrible old Harry was making trouble to feel himself alive, but he stirred others to be angry too. There was an ugliness now in this group of gardeners, with whom Walter had felt at peace; there was a new level of hostility rising in the air; the imagined stranger was a threat that united them.

'We've had things moved,' Harry went on. 'My wheelbarrow was gone from the back of the shed. I found it later, but it had been used. There's someone here. It's dangerous, that's what it is.'

Freddie turned to Walter. 'You thought you saw a man once, have you seen him again?'

Walter was uncomfortable. He had something to hide. He needed to stay quiet and give no one the chance to guess at what he knew. He gave what he hoped was a non-committal, not-quite-a-lie shrug. Before Freddie could quiz him further, Harry went on, 'There's someone alright. Things are being moved; someone's been behind my shed; we had the theft of Sue's pears, all the crop gone in one go.' The dispute gathered pace.

'That's organised; it's not a homeless person doing that.'

'There's plenty of them on the streets if you haven't noticed.'

'They've no right to be on our land. It's not safe.'

'I don't feel safe, knowing someone comes at night – it's creepy.'

'How are they getting in? The new padlock on the gate is secure.'

'Oh, you want to go up the top and have a look. Anyone determined can get over that fence; it's broken in several places. The council said they would fix it last year, nothing done.'

'No money, that's the trouble.'

Lovely Sue had arrived, looking cuddly in a red beret at an angle and a yellow padded coat. He was pleased to see she was not joining in the volume of complaint but standing a little aside, waiting like him for the meeting to begin. He nodded to her, and she grinned back. He had helped her cover up some of her patch for the winter, pulling the heavy cloth over and pinning it down with stones. He knew she could have managed by herself, but she had graciously accepted his offer. Her plot was a patchwork, no straight lines, higgledy-piggledy was the word that came to him. She put flowers among her beans. She was not a messy shape herself, no, she was a satisfyingly compact body, no line out of place. He had asked her about the harvest of pears which she had lost to a thief. She smiled, sighed it off, it was her fault, not putting a padlock on the shed, she had learnt a lesson. 'A hard lesson for a new-timer,' he sympathised.

'Ask me, it's an illegal immigrant. They're all coming in now,' Harry pronounced, unwilling to let the juice go out of his current obsession. 'Someone should report him.'

'Why do you say that?' Freddie asked. 'You've no evidence.'

'Do we even know there is a person on the plots?' Sue asked.

'I saw someone, dark, a foreigner, I'm certain me.' Heads nodded. Everyone knew that the wave of people from all over the world was flowing into the country and the papers said these people were illegal.

Walter felt a tremor of alarm. Was this true? Had the boy been seen? He'd have to tell him to be careful. He was doing no harm, but Walter could not say so now.

Another voice joined in, 'Yes, I think someone's here. My wheelbarrow has been moved again. I didn't see anyone, but I agree, there is someone here.'

'It'll be a man, won't it, but we can manage. If it's an illegal, maybe we could get a group to catch him and throw him out, tell him to go.'

With delight, Harry now said, 'And not come back. I'll lead it. I'm not afraid of some darkie, some gyppo type.'

Freddie intervened. 'We don't need that kind of language please. That is not, please don't. And anyway, we do not know who this person is or might be.' Harry was rebuked but hardly regretful, Walter thought. There were mutterings as if the threat to catch the intruder was real.

Glyn asked Freddie to read out the topics on her agenda so that they would know what was coming. In her deep voice, holding the boy's hand, she told them they were there to discuss the takeover from the council by an eco group, joint purchase of manure and chippings, who would organise bonfire night next week and also the possibility, raised by Harry, that there was someone sleeping at the back of his shed.

In the rambling discussion, elongated despite the weather and lateness of the day by inconclusive statements and vague suggestions, Glyn kept to his usual clarity. What was the problem, what could they do about it, when would it happen? The eco group had expressed an interest, but no one knew more. Freddie undertook to ask the councillor to pursue the situation and keep them informed. Sue asked a question about manure and chippings. Freddie was organising those as well. The bonfire night was Glyn's department. He had started a huge pile of prunings and rubbish from his patch. He would light it; everyone would bring food; there would be money in the kitty for fireworks, only a few because of the danger insisted Freddie, and others agreed; the real aim was to get rid of everyone's untidy bits of sticks and the large dried-out weeds.

Walter shuffled his feet and kept glancing over his shoulder.

In his jacket pocket, wrapped in foil, he had a stilton pasty, warm against his leg. He had planned a large sausage roll with gravy for himself, but this man did not eat meat, not his kind of meat at least. So he had rolled out the pastry into individual pies, one for each of them, filled with leeks softened in butter, then stilton crumbled in. His was waiting at the house; this one he intended to leave on the bench once they were all leaving.

'You will come to the bonfire.' Sue's gentle voice startled him.

'You bet. I will make parkin, perhaps.'

'That would be delicious. You are such a talented baker.' Her enthusiasm was a balm, a little delight. He was conscious that he was almost blushing, though it was too dark for her to see.

'Thank you again for all your help, Walter. See you soon.' She was gone. Glyn and Freddie were trying to make the meeting finish. The rumbling about the "illegal" was hard to suppress. At last Glyn offered to have a patrol around every night.

'Why don't I do that?' Walter found his voice in time. He was worried that Harry would start beating around the hedges, armed with a stick. 'I am the one who lives the closest, well nearly, and I am not working like you, Glyn, and you have family, lots of you do. I will do the patrol. I will be here anyway most likely; it's no trouble to me, it's fine.' He was rambling.

'But it is winter coming, Walter, it is not fair to ask you.' Frederica hesitated, unspoken words hovering in the air. He smiled, stepped forward into the centre of the group, showing his strong shoulders, his lean frame; now they could see he was not only happy to be here every day, but the role was one he fitted. It was only a pity that Sue had already left and was not here to see him take charge.

No one else had definitely seen or spoken to an intruder, but the mutterings, the nastiness of their fear and disapproval had risen into the air, spread like a cloud or mist lying above the decaying plant life. Walter heard someone every time he was here, complaining, speculating, peering with intent as if there was a person lurking at each corner, behind every bush or shed. If there was any actual sign, Harry might be encouraged to form a search party, would be pleased to form an allotment holders lynch group of some kind, ridiculous though that idea was. He worried that, in time, there would be an organised attempt to find Osama and make him leave.

The meeting was glad now to have the matter settled, and it was certainly time for home.

'I'm off, old chap, walk up with me?' Glyn tapped his arm.

'Might as well start as I mean to go on. You get off; I will do my first patrol.'

'There's no real need, is there? All getting their knickers in a twist about a few bits and pieces moved about. I don't even think there is anyone sleeping here. The homeless wouldn't walk this far out of the centre; they need doorsteps and to be close to the Baptist church which offers floor space if it drops below freezing. It's probably urban foxes. There's just so much at the moment on the news and in the papers isn't there, about immigrants, migrants I should say, as if they are likely to make it from Calais to up north here.'

Walter waved with grim cheerfulness as Freddie finally pulled the gate behind her, the last to go, her son dragging his feet and refusing to help carry the cups. Now at last he could find Osama and give him the pasty in person.

Walter walked along the path, toured around the plots, especially near to Sue's shed.

It was cold and dreary; there were no stars; and the moon was clouded. He did not have a torch. His hands were cold. He risked one call out, the man's name a soft sound in the darkness.

He left the pasty on the bench, still glancing around, hoping, seeing nothing.

EIGHT

The sausage rolls, seasoned with sage and onion, golden in his own flaky pastry, are piled satisfyingly high; the roasted ham gleams; the bread rolls are crisp, the salads cheerfully red and green. The two cakes he has made as dessert are waiting in the fridge, a baked cheesecake sweet with vanilla and topped with a sharp compote of the last blackcurrants from the freezer and a dense chocolate cake, gluten free because Celia told him she cannot eat gluten, covered with cream and the last of his frozen raspberries. A feast everyone arriving exclaimed over. Gabby did suggest she could order in pizzas, save him the work, she would pay, everyone loves pizzas. *Not in my house.*

The work has kept him occupied for two days and used up the budget he had set aside. The swell of welcomes, Ry Cooder in the front room just audible, beer bottles fizzing, the fridge door popping open as the white wine is taken out, now Walter can breathe out. The usual suspects have turned up, Frank rubbing his face and his wife Janet in the kitchen, clustered with Gerry; Glyn is here; the wives have gathered; talk is flowing; the bunting Gabby insisted on is ridiculous but somehow helps the atmosphere.

It is a disappointment that he could not invite Sue. He had almost done it, stopped to chat after the bonfire night, asked her if she liked parties, he was on the brink of saying, 'Why don't you pop in, only round the corner, did you know I live on St John's? It's a birthday do.' That had stopped him. He did not want her to be reminded how old he is.

'Good do, mate, and great food. You are a bit of a dark horse, aren't you?' Frank surely knows that Walter started learning to cook for himself when Marie left. It is easy to impress people, it seems. Of course, to be honest with himself, he had intended to impress.

He wants to get Celia alone. He can see her being very outgoing, greeting, hugging even. She is so like her mother to look at but without Linda's softness. She is even thinner today than the last time he saw her. She was a chubby child but is now this angular person, her hair a strict blonde sheet, her clothes expensive, tailored, slightly masculine to his eye. She has had partners, some of whom he has met over the years. She is single now, childless, and in his house acting the part of the favoured daughter as hostess. He knows she is claiming that place in front of Gabby who only lived here briefly. But Gabby is like her mother, who is mercifully absent; she is not to be ignored. She is in the kitchen, urging people to go and fill their plates, finding serving spoons, encouraging the first cutting of the ham into pink slices. He must go to Celia, pull her away from the next-door neighbours, make her talk to him.

Now there is a bit of a stir in the party air; the lights in the dining room are being switched off. He sees that in the kitchen doorway, Gabby and Celia are together, oddly the dark head with the fair. Everyone has stopped talking; there is a hesitation, a ripple of uncertainty.

Celia comes first, bearing a long pie, a pork pie with his name on it spelt out in pastry and the dreaded number, the seven noughts spelt out. She has put candles down its length.

'Your birthday cake, Dad, your favourite, specially made by the butcher.' There are gasps and laughs.

'And you will have to have lots of breath, Walter, here is the sweet cake! Lots of candles.'

Despite his own provision of cakes, Gabby has bought a huge blue and white rectangle, with his name and again, the number. Politely people exclaim over this too. There is to be no escape. To general clapping and a repeat rendition of the birthday song, he blows out one, then two sets of candles. He manages to catch Celia and holds her close for a moment. 'Thank you, love, that is special.' She twists away, starts chatting to the woman next door whom he had not wanted to invite.

Gabby is cutting both the pie and the cake, handing out plates. His men friends start to queue for the pork pie.

'Any news on that problem on your allotments?' Walter hesitates. How did Frank know about that?

Gerry joins in. 'Are you sure it isn't some junkie finding it safer than the streets?'

Outside the bus station in town, a homeless man sits on the ground most days unless it is very wet. There are others; there are sleeping nests in doorways; it is a new shifting population. They have become part of the townscape, each one a normal sight, something to avert your eyes from, but no more than that. The bus shelter man is always in the same spot against the wall. Many do stop to throw him a coin. Walter bought him a takeaway coffee last week, guilty that he is offering food to one and not to this home-grown example.

Bernie heard them. 'What's this, a vagrant on your plot? Is it an illegal? Asking for asylum. As if. What they want is more money, better lives over here. We should send them all back straight away, no question.'

The papers were full of brown people in overcrowded boats at sea and some politicians had started to talk of hordes. Walter thinks of Glyn's "from Calais to here". How little he and his friends know. He is still researching the asylum question. He knows now that their town has a large "distribution centre" for new asylum seekers; he knows that if they are refused, these people are put onto the streets, not allowed to work or claim benefits.

He tries to say something, to make some kind of representation of the facts, to represent the man he has met, the person who is here. But he cannot admit what he knows.

'Why are you so interested all of a sudden?' Bernie says.

'It is not sudden, it is all over the papers, the news, the camps, people in boats, drowning. It is a question of humanity.' He has surprised himself saying so much.

Bernie is silenced. Gerry turns the music up, Dire Straits now, the noise of random conversation rises with it. Walter likes parties when you do not have to talk, and the dancing takes over. Some of the women are collecting in the centre of the sitting room, waiting for the right tune to inspire them. He sees Celia is alone for the moment.

'Hi, how are you doing? The pie, that was such a great idea. When did you ask the butcher?'

'Glad you like it, Dad. I know how much you and your mates like pork pie. It is a good party. Did Gabby organise it all for you?'

'No, I organised it.' He struggles to find the form of words that will help her. 'Gabby started me off, but that's it.'

As soon as he had been persuaded by his stepdaughter to celebrate this milestone, he rang Celia and tried to make it sound as if it was all his own idea. She had not promised to come at first. She rang only the week before to say she could make it. Now she was making what sounded like an accusation.

'I told you I decided to give it a go. And I'm so pleased you could come.'

'I'm not going to stay the night.' She indicates the glass of juice she is holding. 'I'll drive back soon.'

'Stay the night, love, you can leave early if you have to but—'

'Work, Dad, it is Friday tomorrow.'

He knows he should have insisted to Gabby that the party would be on a Saturday. She was full of the notion that it was important to have it on his actual day. He feels a spurt of fury at her.

'Don't see much of you these days. When are you going to come and see your old dad again?' The old is supposed to be jokey, but he sounds weak and sad to his own ears.

'I thought Marie would be here. Surely she couldn't keep away. Is she coming at the weekend? Gabby'll stay till then, won't she?'

He would like to grab her, hold her as if she was a little girl and squash his love into her bones. He can say nothing; how can he reassure her without sounding dishonest? He and Marie can be civil, they maintain an interest in each other, nothing more. And why would it matter so to his daughter if it were more, if he and his ex-wife were still lovers? Marie has suggested to him more than once that they could be, with a wry smile of invitation. What would happen if he brought the lovely Sue along to meet Celia as a new woman in his life? If only.

'Marie was not invited, Celia.'

'Come on, Walter, time for you to dance.' Janet is tugging his arm.

'We are waiting.' Gabby appears, face flushed, eager to entice him to join them. Walter has a reputation as one of the few men who will dance. He is secretly proud of this. He still loves to get lost to the music, to feel his body move in different ways. He could have been a dancer, someone once told him that. Not a planner but a dancer!

Celia is releasing him, despite his reluctance, shrugging, smiling falsely at Gabby, letting him go. When he turns from the dance, three songs later, he is determined to find her. In the hallway, he sees her with her coat.

'Don't stop, Dad, you're having a good time. Why not at your great age, haha.'

'Celia, give me a ring. Come and have lunch with me, or I'll come to you. We must talk about Christmas.'

She is gone; the door closes.

When the last revellers are leaving, twenty minutes after that unseen message has passed from mind to mind saying it is time to go, Walter stands for a moment on the doorstep, the goodbyes echoing down the street. Behind him the house will need clearing and cleaning. Gabby has filled the dishwasher with glasses, but the kitchen tops are covered in debris. The remains of his feast are in the fridge, carefully rescued and covered by Janet. 'Enough here for the weekend, at least, Walter. You won't have to cook again.'

Out in the cold night, along the street, around the corner and a few more yards, the dark wilderness of the allotments is waiting. A man is going to sleep against a hedge of brambles, with the wooden side of a shed for safety.

What can I do? he thinks. *I can't help him. I can't even help Celia. That's who I should be worried about.*

'A night cap?' Gabby is curled on the sofa, drinking brandy, ready to discuss everyone who came, to chew over the evening's details for pleasure.

'You did well, a great party. Clap on the back.'

He has to smile; her warmth reaches out to him. But he goes to bed, resisting her, feeling the backwash, his mind full of conflicts, knowing he needs the oblivion of sleep.

NINE

Freddie pulled the branch gently down towards him.

'Here, see the buds either face inwards or, like this one, outwards. That is what you want. You need a good clean cut just above there.'

Walter followed her finger. He would not have realised that the tiny shape on the bough was a bud, an opportunity for new growth. He used the secateurs with care, cutting off the two-foot length she recommended.

'A little ragged,' she said. 'Look, I'll clean it up like this. Try to make the next one more sloping, then the rain flows off, you see.'

She reached up for another branch. He thought how her hands touched the tree as if the bark might be feeling her touch. She stroked a branch with careful fingers, almost tenderly. She looked, considered, took in the whole before she made suggestions.

'These are not in bad shape, Walter. You have had good crops and there is quite a bit of new growth. You have given them a mulch of manure, well done.'

'But they are getting straggly.'

'Yes, it is a good idea to tidy them up. You don't want them too tall; you won't be able to pick the fruit.'

He was conscious of how close they were standing, how unconcerned this young woman was by his shoulder almost rubbing hers. Her arm showed muscular strength against his own sinewy thinness. She was thoughtfully responding only to the tree, conscious of each twig, each curve of a branch, not to the man breathing by her side.

'Trees are all different. You will get to know their habits.'

He had never thought of trees having habits. Inside his gloves his fingers stung with cold.

'Trees will forgive you if you make a mistake.' He raised his eyebrows. Trees forgive? 'Just do a little at a time, not too much this year, don't be in a hurry.'

The lesson was over. She turned for her own plot, satisfied with the morning's work.

'How did you learn all this?'

She grinned at him. 'Time and effort. Plus, my dad was an orchard keeper once upon a time.'

He wanted to ask her more, to stop her leaving his side, but she had finished with him. So, too old for her interest, sadly. *You don't do bad for your age*, he thought. Look okay in the mirror. But she's a young woman, on the other side of the fence of years. Her hair is a marvel of nature. He stood, stamping his feet in the cold, looking at the apple trees. The stone fruits, as she called them, would have to wait until summer, but he had learnt enough to tackle the task. He had inherited this square of fruit trees when he took on the allotment. He had not been able to name any of the varieties until this eco girl appeared with her beauty and a child at the knee or the breast. Walter, my boy, you have fallen for a Viking. You admire her.

He gathered the cuttings he had made so far. It was too cold to continue. He would come back tomorrow. His roses at the edge of the plot and the few left at home needed pruning too; it was time for a fire in the old dustbin.

On the bench, the flask of spicy vegetable soup was a query and a concern. He had left it the evening before, full, with a clearly written label. When Frederica saw it this morning, she asked him directly what it was. 'My lunch, just because it is so cold today. Would you like some?' This was a risk as he had checked it and knew it was still full, but he was not sure it was warm enough to match his story. 'No, thanks, I have to get back, can't leave the baby for too long with my mother.'

So his offering had not been taken, had been left again. Yesterday's ginger cake had been uneaten, sitting lonely and staling in its tin. For three days the food had been untouched.

From that first night of the pastry, he had cooked with the young man in mind, a double portion of whatever he fancied himself or had the ingredients for: vegetable stews for the damp and cold, thick soups with chunks of bread, an occasional cake, the extra scones on Saturday. If he timed his "patrol" carefully, he would often find Osama waiting for him. They sat on the bench for a short while and talked quietly, of the weather as English people do; slowly Walter allowed himself to ask more questions, always careful to pitch them lightly.

'You must miss your family?'

'It is hard. I ring my mother every week. She says, son, are you fine? I say, yes I am fine.'

Osama dropped his head. 'What else can I say? I am alone here.'

'But you have friends here, in the town. You were sleeping at a friend's, before?'

Walter could see that the man had other sources of support. He was clean even though he slept outside. He stayed smart, had a scarf now it had begun to be properly cold.

'There are many of us, you know. The ones with nothing, who are not allowed to have anything, to work, to live a life.' Walter stared at the man. 'I know some people. Sometimes a friend is not so good.'

He told Walter that he had tried to get the Home Office to recognise him. He had had the help of a solicitor, but his asylum claim had been refused twice.

'But, you know, it is hard. I can't work here. I can't have a life. I came here for this? Very hard.' He seemed to shrink as he said this, sitting in the chill of evening, on a garden bench on someone else's land. Mostly when he spoke to Walter he looked resigned, calm. But these words rang in Walter's head. He had no way of answering. He did not know how to help. Even so many of the allotment holders who were generous with their ideas, advice and produce too when there was a glut, even these people who Walter knew and liked, even they would not want to see this man here, taking up their space without permission or licence. As he thought this, Walter glanced around, checking again that they were alone, no one had come in.

There had been more scenes of protests at the border of the Gaza Strip. It was reported that Israel was arming itself with snipers against their opponents, who were young men in bandannas, hurling rocks. Osama had not said he had participated in this kind of action. Five years ago, was that even happening? Walter could not remember. He had not followed closely this branch of international news.

Sometimes Osama seemed vacantly hopeless, as if he could not speak of it anymore. Loss seeped out of him, a sense of unspoken hurt like a mist spreading into the dark air. Walter felt it creep inside him sitting there. He was nervous to ask questions that went too close. He did not ask how he had travelled here. If he arrived five years ago, the Calais camp had still been there. Not a camp, a kind of jungle, named as such, a collection of makeshift temporary tents and shelters among the trees, people hiding in mud and rubbish, waiting for the chance to cross the Channel. Walter thought of the scenes on the television of the French guards patrolling the fences, the young escapees in the dark trying to get onto the back of a lorry, failing but trying again the next night. His mind flinched at the case of several men freezing to death in a locked container, the details too terrible for him to absorb. Now the camp had been demolished; there was little reporting about those who had been using it as a home. Walter wanted to know, and also not to know, how this companion in the winter evening had arrived at his own piece of land, in a lorry, under the Eurostar train, or in a tiny boat swamped with the dangerous waters of the Channel.

He tried to think of topics about his own life that would interest Osama or lighten their minutes together. He talked about what he was growing, pointing out what was in the earth, kale surviving the chill, late spinach. The man took an interest in Walter's plans.

'In my country we do not grow this stuff for people, only for animals.' He pointed at the kale. 'Lots of spinach we have. You have good apples here. A pity there are no lemons.'

Walter realised he was being teased. 'No lemons,' he agreed solemnly. 'We have to buy those. I would love to pick a lemon from a tree. That's a special thing.'

'Not so special to us. Important though. We have a lot; we use them a lot. Have you ever had a preserved lemon? In a jar? No, you must try.'

Occasionally, Walter mentioned his daughter, where she lived, how old she was. He did not speak of his lost Linda or his second marriage. He did not say that his daughter was a solicitor.

'We had a pomegranate tree in our garden,' Osama said one evening. 'They are beautiful, you know. My mother used the fruit for lots of things, so many meals.'

Walter wondered what such a tree would look like. He remembered as a child being given the strange fruit as a one off treat – you squeezed the hard pinkish skin slowly in your hands, rolling it around until the pips inside were softened. Then you made a hole and drank the juice, sharp and sweet together and slightly bitter from the pith. He had no idea how you would use that juice or those pips for cooking, though he had seen cooks on the television scattering the pips for decoration. It had seemed to him a silly, fanciful addition to savoury dishes.

'Your mother was a good cook.' Not a question.

'I remember the smell of food at home, her food. Yes, the smell. It does not smell like that here. Sometimes I have food which is sort of the same but never the smell. I miss smell.'

There were lots of questions to ask about the food from Osama's country. There would be other evening talks, so many things to hear and say. But the time on the bench was short, a brief session that he always needed to end, to say goodnight and leave the man there. Because he knew there was a barrier he must keep in place; he must not get too involved and no one must know the man was here. The secret of these meetings had to remain under the hedges with Osama's bedroll.

Taking food down to the bench gave Walter a new purpose, a reason to consult Linda's recipe file or the food programmes on the television, a pleasant sense of interest in his shopping, the carrier bag heavier on his arm as he walked home through the bus station. At this dead part of the year, when he could only spend a small portion of every day working on his plot, and the shortened days closed him so much into the house, he still felt active, useful. He looked forward to his night-time trip down to the allotments, unlocking the gate quietly, stepping onto the grass by the shed, looking to see if there was a figure waiting for him. If there was no one, he would wait a little, deciding he was early or too late, reluctant to leave the food without a conversation but knowing the cold would drive him away before long. Last night he had taken a hot water bottle filled to the brim and an extra blanket. Each night as he took himself to the warm nest of his own bed, he asked the same questions: *Why did I start this? What can I do? What help can I really give? I am not the kind of person to make a difference here.*

On this December morning, he took the flask and the hot water bottle back home. The soup was still warm when he emptied it into the saucepan for his lunch.

TEN

Her hands wrapped in a tea towel, Celia picked up the green vegetable dish he had placed at one end, putting the potato one nearer to the middle, rearranging the hot dishes on the table he had carefully laid with his food. She caught his glance. For a second, she hesitated, and he saw her lack of confidence, her insecurity, in dealing with him.

'Okay, Dad, any way you like. I just think it is prettier, more orderly, like this.

'It's fine. We are going to eat it, however it looks.' This sounded a little too sharp. 'The food is ready, so is the table; come on, love, time to sit and raise a glass.'

Father and daughter toasted each other with the traditional "here's to us". Walter wondered who now was us. He included Gabby in his mental picture, outsider though she might be. He feared Celia only meant this small presence, the two of them, surrounded by the paraphernalia of Christmas, the room softened by tea lights and the glitter of unopened crackers. It had been Linda who created the atmosphere, brought in the spirit, laughing as she went from crowded stove to crowded table, always inviting her parents and his old dad, making sure they had people around them. The holiday with Marie, Gabby and Celia had been a different kind of hectic, with lots of Marie's relatives whom he and Celia hardly knew.

Gabby had been on the phone a week ago.

'Howdy, Stepdad. We haven't talked about Christmas. You and Celia will be on your own. Why don't you come over to Mum's? It'll be chummy for us all. Come on, say you will. It'll be fine. Mum says it will be fine. She will cook; you can drink, a taxi home – why not?'

He had not told Celia about this offer. He had experienced too many riotous occasions at Marie's new home, too many loud affairs when he had drunk too much to be able to rescue Celia from Gabby's overenthusiastic chats.

Today they were alone, as he had chosen. He wanted to give them time together, to be with her, to see her relax and enjoy herself. There was a heavy quiet now in the room. The ceremony was empty. They needed something which was not there.

'Come on now, you are so thin, you can squeeze in another roastie.'

'No, thank you. I am full. And please don't comment on my weight every time I see you.'

The tartness in her voice lingered like a stain as she gathered dishes and cleared food. How could it be like this between them? He had failed with his precious girl, his only, darling, child. What had he done that she blamed him so? He had married Marie too soon, he could say that. But he had never stopped loving Linda or Celia herself. He had been so lonely. Did she know that?

The rest of the day lay ahead.

'Are you going to flame the pudding now or later. Shall we wait a bit?'

'Let's wait. Please come and sit down. Let me tell you something.'

'That sounds serious.' There was a flicker of confusion or unease in her pale face.

'Well, it is in a way. But not personally.'

For six weeks, Walter had patrolled the site with increasing concern. Had Osama been driven out, not by a mob, but by the hostility of people, a collective breath of opposition coming from plot holders, horrified by his presence. The bundle was in the shed, hidden behind the wheelbarrow, as he had told Osama it would be. He had added to it with a sleeping bag and a pillow. It was a reproach to him, a dry but inadequate outdoor bedroll. Each evening he took a torch to check all the places behind sheds, under fruit trees, up against the top fence, searching and hoping for a sign. The man, the boy as Walter thought of him, had gone. There were no clues, no tracks, no traces.

Anxious and frustrated, one dark afternoon Walter looked again for information about asylum seekers and the UK law. It became compulsive. Every day he reread the official immigration rules and statements, scanned the news items. There was a flood of people coming towards Europe, searching, thousands and thousands of them, for refuge and escape. So many with nowhere to go. Camps filling up on borders. Fences being built to keep them out. And a very small percentage of those who flee start on a route which ends on a British coast. Trying to get here to this cold place where it seems no one wants them, where they are called illegals, he thought so often in wonder and confusion. Typing the words "Palestinian refugees" brought no information at all.

Celia was waiting calmly for him to begin. So, he cleared his throat.

'There is a young man. An asylum seeker.' He knew the correct use of the term now. 'His name is Osama.'

Celia was startled. She thought I was going to say something about Gabby and Marie perhaps; who knows what had gone through her mind, nothing like this.

'I have met him because he has been… he was sleeping rough on the allotments.'

'So all those people at your party last month! They were right. You have got an intruder on there.'

Walter thought he had not heard so much talk at the party, or perhaps he had forgotten conversations half heard.

'He is not an intruder. He is a person, in trouble.'

'Why is he sleeping rough? If he is an asylum seeker, the law allows him accommodation and an allowance. Not much but for the basics.'

'He has been refused.'

'So he is not an asylum seeker. He is an illegal immigrant.'

She was using a clipped professional tone. She had heard his sympathy for the boy and was intent on stamping it out. They were opposing each other, on different sides.

'I haven't seen him for a couple of weeks. But I am hoping he is alright and maybe he will be back.' She looked at him with a cold eye. He could spoil their time together if he continued.

'Let's do the pudding. I can tell you more when we have

eaten all the rum butter.' His grandmother had made all the Christmas puddings for the family of aunts and uncles when he was a child. Theirs had arrived in a thick white basin, wrapped with a headscarf of white cloth. This was a poor substitute in its black plastic pot, he always thought, even when Linda supplied it. He did not have a large family waiting for such a gift, so this was one culinary art he had not tried to learn. The pagan tribute seemed a lonely flame in its bath of brandy, warmed on a spoon with the required reverence. He sliced them both a very small piece. *The best is in the sauces*, he thought, as with lots of food; this rich, fruity thing needs its silky cream and the punch of alcohol in the butter to go down.

'How come you know this man's name?'

'I've met him; we've talked. I've given him food sometimes, leftovers I can't manage.' This was an untruth, but he would not admit more. 'It was very cold in October this year, when I first met him.' He was justifying himself under her gaze.

'You know you should not do that.'

'Do I? Know that?' He met her challenge directly.

'Okay, it's humanitarian of you.'

'And we are not yet Hungary in this country. Or in this house.' She kept her head down, her eyes away from his.

Quietly, they began to move to the more comfortable venue of the sitting room, taking the chocolate mints with them. Now was the ritual time for the Scrabble game but neither moved to open the box. He offered her another glass of port. She refused but Walter poured himself a satisfying glug.

'Osama is Palestinian. He is young, about thirty. He doesn't know his exact date of birth.'

Celia acknowledged with a nod that this was not unusual in some other countries.

'You know about the situation in Gaza. Of course you do. So his family sent him here for safety.' He did not say that was five years ago and since then he has been working to survive, hidden and unseen by the official radar. He is surprised by how proud he feels that he had gained Osama's trust. He has listened to him, both sitting side by side on the bench by the shed; he has listened to him talk of his parents, their anxiety, their pain at losing him but their insistence that he must go in order to be safe.

'What has he been doing? Before he ended up on your allotment, being fed by you all that time?'

'Trying to claim asylum. He has failed twice because he doesn't have the papers.'

'He has failed twice?'

'He can't get the papers as there is no Palestinian embassy in the UK. The Home Office refuses to accept that the papers he has got are genuine.'

'He has been refused, more than once. So he is homeless. Has he had a letter saying he will be deported? You know that's the next step. And the best one, really, for him I mean. To go home.'

Walter was shocked at her careless assumption that deportation was acceptable. But an instinct of restraint came to him. He had hoped for her warmth, that she would respond as he had done to the plight of a stranger. He had intended to bring her closer. He had planned today to ask about her, to know more about her work, about her friendships, to risk the topic of her emotional life. He knew she had had several relationships that did not last. He had wondered if it would be a woman that brought her happiness at last. Now he was trapped in this problem of his own, this new obsession in his mind.

'I am worried about him, that's all. He might be in trouble. There's been no sign of him.'

'The problem has gone away then.' She saw his disappointment at this brisk summation.

'He might be in one of those terrible detention centres.'

'But he might not. Nothing you can do about it if he is, Dad.'

'But people get stuck in them. For nothing, for ages.'

'Dad, it is the system.'

Unable to challenge this, anxious to reclaim the day, he said, 'Come on, it is Scrabble time.'

As she was putting out the board and rattling the pieces in the bag, she looked at her father and smiled. He knew it was a gift.

'You have been kind, Dad, as always. Well done. It's a harsh world. Perhaps he has found a better refuge. You have done what you could.'

ELEVEN

He continues to click onto websites for refugee information most days. He reads the case study of a man who was teaching in Kuwait and was imprisoned because of his statements about equality of race and birth. He dodges the descriptions of how this man was tortured. Another post discusses the cases of people separated from their families, losing fathers, wives, children on their journey as refugees. Or of those who were forced to leave them behind in the urgency of peril. Professions and possessions abandoned in flight. He reads of a doctor who fled Afghanistan and waited three years before he was given approval to stay. He now practises in a British hospital. He studies the picture of a young black face, a man from Sudan who is waiting in hope for his younger brother to escape a refugee camp and join him. A calm-looking, open face. He cannot imagine what truth and experience lies behind it. There is information about the statistics, the law, the harshness of the asylum system in the UK, which sites call "tough" and "hostile". There are many groups involved in action and protest. Planes are being grounded by protesters who try to stop deportations of vulnerable people back to these terrible circumstances they have fled. His head is filling up with these stories and facts. A sense of helpless anger rises in him; there is nothing to be done. He can do nothing.

There is no sign of his own invader on the allotment; his asylum seeker is absent.

When the Israeli situation is on the news, he is fixed, listens, tries to understand – occupation, rocket launches, barriers and settlements. He has never asked Osama any details about all this.

You do what you can. That's it, nothing more to be said. Nothing more you can do. Here in this house, in this ordinary street in a northern city, one man, one house, one street, and stretching out from here beyond the known boundaries, there is a system grinding up individuals who have been bold enough, desperate enough, to step in front of it. Walter is of no significance, is helpless, unable to pull the stop lever.

He looks at his neighbours, at passers-by in the city, in car parks and shops; he sees what he had not paid attention to before, that there are new faces in the town. He sees young Africans in pairs and groups, tall men in trendy jackets, holding phones to their ears as they walk. There are Arab men too, dark-eyed with beards. They look foreign but modern all these, the same as everyone else in town, except for something in their movements, a hesitation in their stride. So many young men, so many Osamas. There are fewer women; some of them are wearing long dresses, soft trousers like the Pakistani community. Only a few are wearing the black cover-up. Some of the African women are tall and striking, beautiful, he thinks. Some are shrinking along the edges, wearing woolly caps on their heads.

He remarks on it to Frank one pub night. 'Never really noticed before how many refugees we have got here. It is the distribution centre, I suppose.' He sounds carelessly knowledgeable. It seems Frank knew this about where they live, that they are one of only five places in the country where asylum seekers are sent at first. He nods into his beer.

'There's a charity now which acts to welcome them, offer friendship, you know, a hand held out, that kind of thing.'

'Some of them are refused, can't work or get benefits. How do they live?'

'Mostly it's people from the churches get involved, but not all of them. I think the Cathedral does a lot too. Janet's talking about joining at the centre they've set up. Volunteering to help out.'

Frank's wife Janet was a quiet woman like her husband, with a cap of dark blonde hair which Walter knew Linda had envied, her own flyaway hair always a misery to her. Janet had a habit as strange and repetitive as the way her husband rubbed his face and nose as if on a timer. With her right hand, she tugged at a section of her hair over her shoulder, pulled it out as if she was going to make bunches, caressed it then smoothed it down slowly. There would be a pause, before her slender fingers sought out a strand from the other side, feeling for it carefully, bringing it round to touch her lips. Back and forth, her fingers searching out, loving her hair section by section. Walter had seen her do this at parties, film nights, even in the pub. He wondered how these two passed evenings, avoiding each other's eyes as each was locked into their repetitions.

Walter ponders what Frank has said. He thinks about going to volunteer too. He could go down to this centre one day and ask them what the situation for Palestinians is; he could see if they know Osama's name. Perhaps he has been to ask for help there. But the days pass. He thinks that Osama will come back to the bench. The figure of the young man haunts him; that jacket he was wearing when they met, a thin material meant for show not warmth, the jeans baggy at the knee, dark eyes startling in a long stubbled face; he is another ghost, glimpsed but never encountered now.

Walter feels he is not a person to help all others. He does not have the energy, the feelings, the hope. It is one young man, with serious brown eyes, who said he, Walter, is like his father, it is his situation which he broods on.

In the blank parts of the day, he reads and absorbs what he can bear, ignores what he cannot. He waits for something to happen. His life has passed in waiting, not in action.

The allotment is a place of dead vegetation, neglect and decay. There is a list of timely winter jobs in his notebook, left unmarked, incomplete. He has spent his working life moving paper, responding to urgent but temporary messages, contributing to decisions long since overridden or permanently delayed. The pattern of growth and renewal on his plot had given him a new sense of connection and belonging. Bent double over the soil, he sometimes thought of his peasant ancestors, ruefully reminding himself that his labour is chosen, not necessary. He is the guardian of the plot's fertility; he feels the power of making it happen. He had listened to Frederica's little lecture to the allotment holders meeting about the importance of soil, regenerative soil she called it, organic and eco-friendly, improving the taste of their produce and the health of the planet. He was pleased to think he contributed in his small way.

But nature is waiting to take back, to seize on neglect, to overcome his control. The notebook list has pushed him forward season after season. He leaves it unopened.

One January day he was startled by Sue appearing at his elbow.

'Hi, Walter. Haven't seen you for ages. It's not been lotty weather, has it? I haven't been near mine. But you are more committed, I think?' She grinned.

She peered with frank curiosity at the selection of trays in his trolley, a neat stack of ready food for the week. She made no comment on what she saw, but he was sure she was surprised by his purchases. Guilty as charged, he thought.

His habit of pleasure in the preparation of meals had left him. For the first time since the year of Linda's death, those empty months when he only stumbled through life, he strolled along the fast food aisles, reading labels for smoked fish pie, duck in plum sauce, spicy baked ribs. He fingered a tray, put it down, tried another. The lurid pictures had no impact, and he could not believe the enticing phrases. He piled plastic randomly into the trolley.

He was silent, unable to find the sentences he needed to make conversation with this lovely woman.

'I don't get much time anyway at the moment. Work's a bit hectic,' she said.

'I have all the time in the world. But there's not much to do there at this time of year.'

'No, just as well. You see my daughter has come home, that's it too.'

'How old is she?'

'Too old to be lying in bed expecting me to run around. Oh, I shouldn't say that should I? It's lovely to have her really. But you know, I have got used to life on my own. They don't think you've got a life, do they, adult children?'

'My daughter is a bit the same. Thinks I have nothing to do. Not that she's come home. She's working away. She's in Manchester, very successful.'

'That's so great. Lucky you. My poor Julie is a mess, boyfriend up and off, no money for the rent he left her with, emotions all over the place. Mum must be the refuge. Parents can't refuse, but between me and you and only us, Walter, I feel very fed up today.'

To Walter's eye she looked far from unhappy. She looked cheerful, composed in her yellow coat. He stood waiting for the right thing to come to him, smiling at her, warmed by her confidence in him. So she lived alone, was divorced probably, a lone soul like him.

'So there you are.' She moved her trolley a little way.

'How about a coffee?' he dared to ask.

'Thanks, how kind you are. Can't though. I must get this lot into the fridge and be ready for work. I do shifts you see, at the hospital. I'm a nurse, you know.'

'Another time,' he murmured as she pushed her shopping away. He did not know she was a nurse; he knew so little about her. She thought him kind.

'Well, once the sun comes out, I'll see you down on the plot.' She moved on, unknowing of the longing which had seized him.

She stopped and turned for a moment, startling him.

'Did you know that there is a lock now on the back fence? Yes, the council have fixed it at last. So we shouldn't have any more professional thieves taking stuff.' She smiled with a rueful look. 'But some people are saying they have seen someone down there, even in this weather. I haven't been, but I heard that.'

Now Walter has a new worry; he has an urgent motive to go down to the patch. Someone else may catch Osama. There could be trouble for the man. That day he jams his shopping bags on the kitchen table and rushes out without changing his shoes. He opens the gate, as quietly as he can, glances up and along the paths, searches along the edges, walks around as if he is without purpose, just strolling, no more. But there is no sign.

Two weeks later the weather has improved; there is sunshine every day; it is a freak warm spell come too early. The swathes of snowdrops he has carefully spread year on year because they were one of Linda's favourites, "they are so brave", those frail markers of a spring yet to come, are sorry. The unseasonal sun has blasted them in a few days so that they hang browned heads. The world is delirious with pleasure. On the TV there are scenes of people sunbathing in parks. It is only February, but it is a record heatwave. Presenters are ecstatic; on the street everyone stops to exclaim to their neighbours; the arrival of summer before spring is to be celebrated. Walter has seen the first pair of shorts in town, large thighs bulging, the T-shirt tight and too short. Soon girls will start dressing as if for the beach when their only destination is the artificial heat of a shop. Walter thinks of the unnatural warming which has caused it and the frosts which will follow this false start. He spends one day clearing brown leaves and dead stalks and gives up. The habitual rhythms he has enjoyed for the years he has lived alone, with his life with Marie over and his daughter and stepdaughter independent and separate, the peaceful pace he gave himself, smugly sure of his worth and his pleasures, these have dissipated. This is the time of year to plan his planting, check his seeds and buy more, with the annual promise of new growth and harvest to come. When he does go to the allotment, now he goes to look, to wait, to hope that there will be a sighting, signs of a return. He is restless, torpid, bored with himself, unable to say why.

The false spring was followed by heavy rain, falling like grey rods, chilling and urgent. He knew the land needed the drink, but each hour was heavy. The slow lifting of light in the morning, the creeping back of dusk closed him in. He forced himself to drive into town for his essentials. In the stale air of the shopping centre, there were few people; the city centre was thinning out, empty shop fronts and to let signs multiplying.

Ahead of him, he saw a tall figure in a blue coat. A man turning to go into the chemists a few feet away. *That is my old coat*; Walter recognised it with a shock. Osama was here. He began to walk faster, then faster, into the shop, searching for the man among the shoppers studying vitamins and hair products on the shelves. There was no sign of him. He must have gone out into the rain. Walter hesitated as the automatic doors opened, put up his collar and stepped out. In both directions, in front of the cathedral, down towards the benches under the trees, he could see no one in a blue coat. After a few minutes of dithering, one way then the other, cold water trickling down his neck, he ducked into the bookshop. Osama was here, had shelter somewhere, was not locked up in a detention centre, was free. Perhaps he would be back to see him; a small flame of hope that Walter would see him soon. Shaking rain from his coat, waiting to broach the weather again so he could double back inside the dry shopping centre, he was warmed by the thought.

TWELVE

He slapped the wheel with his left hand in frustration. The traffic was slowing again; the overhead signs said "Incident"; and the permitted speed limit dropped by another ten miles an hour. He would be late. He fumbled to see what music he had, but the only CD was the latest Bob Dylan which Frank had given him for his birthday, and that low growl did not fit his mood. He switched the radio on and off. Today he could not tolerate the usual political to-ing and fro-ing. At last, the river of metal began to pick up speed. They were coming up to the stretch of road over the moor, the highest motorway in the country. At one point, the road divided to leave a farmhouse in the middle – the story was that the farmer refused to take the money he was offered to sell to the road developers. If it was true, the roar of traffic on either side of its narrow patch must make life unsupportable there. Saddleworth at the top was a bare, inhospitable expanse stretching away into the horizon, with its dark history, a buried child, a despairing mother, a killer immune to human agony. The papers still raised the story sometimes. This part of the drive gave him a fleeting chill.

Now it was down into the city, and he had to remember which was her junction; despite the many times he had driven this route, he was always unsure. Enter the city the wrong way and you could be turning right and left in a circle, led by signs that gave no true direction. Celia's flat was in what had been the old post office, a central building now converted and desirable for its location. He intended to take Celia for lunch, to a pub within walking distance. You went downstairs to a comfortable gloom where they served slabs of pie and a good pint. She would want wine, of course. But Celia brushed off his apology for lateness and his suggestion that they set off straight away. 'There's no need to go out, Dad. We can eat in. I am ready for you.'

He sat and watched as she started to lay the tiny table with food from the fridge. Her hair was different, the strands thicker, with a tumbled look. She was wearing those heavy laced-up shoes he thought of as being men's but more shiny. He thought she looked happier, less tense than so often.

'You okay, Dad? Hungry? I won't be long.'

He smiled and shook his head. He would have to wait for the right moment to talk to her. Let her be hostess for now.

'Come on then. Help yourself.'

She cut thick slices of bread that had a hard, chewy crust and holes in the dough. He stared at small plates and bowls of cold food, all kinds of deli foods, small fish, wrinkled tomatoes in oil, odd-coloured cheeses, the kind of sharp leafed salad that stuck in your teeth. His pie and pint was lost. 'Fill your plate, Dad.' She had been shopping for him, was offering the kind of foods she considered luxurious.

'This is a treat,' he affirmed.

When he could no longer select anything more, she told him to go up onto the overhead floor which he thought of as an indoor balcony but had a fancy name. The sofa was up there, her bedroom and the bathroom off to one side. He did so while she cleared up, refusing his help. She brought up coffee in very small cups.

'I have something to tell you.'

Her announcement cut across his intention to ask her what she knew about detention centres and what happened to people once they had been taken in. He demurred. 'You first, it doesn't matter, it's not important.'

'I am going to have IVF. In fact, I have started it.'

He knew his mouth was open, his eyes fixed. He felt his heart thud as if he had been hit. All he could say at first was "my goodness", several times.

She was ready with her statements. 'Look at me, Dad. I am thirty-five. If I want children, I have to go ahead. This is the only way. The only way for me now.'

'I get one free go on the NHS and then I have to pay. So be it. I earn good money.'

He wanted to ask about Rick, a name he had heard before Christmas. She had said she was going to see him at New Year. So that relationship had not worked.

'How will you manage?'

'How does anyone?' There was little he could find to say. On your own, no sleep, work, childcare, how to cope when the child screams – they whirled around in his head and the room but were unspoken. He knew he had coped as a parent because Linda was calm and patient and he went to work. Gratefully.

'But this flat?' He gestured at the smart small space with its logical layout and restricted furniture. 'You will have to get a pram up those stairs into the building.'

'There is a lift,' she answered. 'So, Dad, you will be a grandparent. The baby's only one.' Her eyes were so intensely focused on him that he had to look away for a blink.

'That will... would be wonderful, love. Your mother would have been so happy. She is happy looking down at you. Sorry if that's silly to you, but I think your lovely mother is still with us. In some ways at least.' To his annoyance, his eyes had filled. He could not say that he saw her sometimes, could he?

'Oh, Dad, don't talk about Mum or I'll cry too,' Celia said quietly.

'Perhaps you and I haven't talked enough about her. Eh?' He could not risk his voice with more. 'Any road up, as they say, if you don't think I am too old, I will help as much as I can.'

'Too old, not you, Dad. Everyone always says how amazing my father is. Looks so young.' She knew this would make him smile with satisfaction. 'You are as fit as anything. You are always on the go.'

He thought of his stiff knees and the new pain in his shoulder. *I'm twice your age*, he reflected; *how big the gap between me and this new life will be.*

'What happens now then?'

'It takes ages, injections, hormones, then the implant. The implants, they always do two. It won't be for a few weeks yet.'

Walter realised that there was one question he had not asked. Who was the sperm donor, how had she found a "father" for this new life? Could she really contemplate two babies without a father to help?

'I have chosen someone to donate the sperm, Dad.' She had seen his confusion. 'It is fine, he is a friend, he has agreed not to interfere with the baby or, if it is successful, the twins. We are going to talk about all that. You don't need to worry.'

As he was leaving, she said, 'Please, don't tell Gabby.'

'Is it a secret?' he replied, knowing that this was not the point.

'Yes, yours and mine, our secret, Dad.'

*

Driving back over the dark moor as dusk blotted out the valley below, where only pinpricks of light showed there was habitation, Walter tried to study his reactions, to grab hold of his feelings about this explosion in his expectations. He could only think of Linda, of her sweet calmness, and her joy at a child, any child she met or saw. She had longed for them to have another one, a sibling for Celia. She told him it was a physical necessity; this longing happened in her body. They waited and she had hoped. He had been happy to have one daughter, did not see the family she imagined. Had she known of his indifference? When it was certain she was dying, a knowledge they could not hide from any longer, as she lay on the sofa only able to drink through a straw, his lissom girl reduced to a bony shadow of a woman, even then she had murmured to him of that loss. Now perhaps there was going to be a child, one which was Celia's and his too, when Linda was not here to see.

THIRTEEN

He tugged at a last parsnip, a muddy misshapen thing, its mandrake roots reluctant to give up their grip. Each twisted tentacle clung to the earth. Walter considered the day he planted the finger-thin seedlings, mild June air, the hope and expectation of parsnips for the Christmas table; now the very last one was an ugly leftover. Frank stood to one side, watching with scepticism on his face.

'What is that?'

'That, my friend, is a parsnip. A splendid one – will make great soup.'

'If you say so, mate. Rather you than me. Is it really worth it, all this bother?'

Frank was waiting for him to finish so that they could go back to the house. He was expecting coffee and cake. Walter considered the vegetable he had dug up. It was his effort that had made this thing, so he would take it home and cook it. But in truth, without Frank there, with his sharp eye and tongue, this one was only fit for the compost heap.

'Right, let me put these tools away and I'll be with you.' He cleaned each carefully, rubbed his hands too, and placed the spade and fork back in their slots inside the shed. As he turned to close the door, he caught a glint from the gap behind. There was a white plastic cup by the bean sticks. A sign. He felt gladness as a shock. He would hurry back tonight. Osama had left him a sign that he was here, was coming back to see him.

Back in the house, as he served the lemon and raspberry loaf he had baked earlier, he was thinking, planning, waiting.

'Have you seen anything more of that trespasser? On the allotments? You haven't mentioned it. Has it all gone quiet then?'

'Well, actually,' he stopped, knife in the air. 'I have seen him. He is a young man, a refugee in fact.' He waited for Frank to respond. He took the chance to trust his old friend who passed his hand thoughtfully over his head as he listened.

'How do you know?'

'I have had a few chats with him. He is an asylum seeker. He comes from, he came from Palestine.' He paused. 'He's got good English. He's a nice lad.'

'Palestine. We don't get many of them in this country. It's mostly Iraqis, Iranians, lots of Africans of course. Janet has never mentioned a Palestinian.'

Walter put a slice of the cake on a plate in front of Frank.

'Delicious, sir, as usual. I don't think I would take up cake baking if Janet, you know, goes, but I'm glad you did, mate.'

'So how have the other plot holders taken this news?' Frank laughed knowingly. 'Have they set up a lynch mob yet?'

'It's only me, no one else has actually seen him. There's been no trouble. But there could be. Some of them, that old boy, he's vicious, and it's fashionable now, isn't it, to be, you know, anti-immigrants.'

'But he's not an immigrant, is he? If he has cause to be a refugee, he can claim asylum. You should tell him to get down to the Sanctuary Centre. They might be able to help him. Has he got an appeal ongoing?'

Walter had no idea.

*

That evening, the light extended now by the turning of the globe and government time management, he took a flask of the parsnip soup with a fresh crusty roll from the shop. He had made a decision. The news of Celia's plan had given him a start. He thought of it as that. He had started again; energy had flooded back into him. Now he could see what needed to be done for the asylum seeker. He would heed Frank's advice and take Osama to the Sanctuary Centre in town, make sure someone looked after him. He would start by inviting him to dinner at the house. He would not be a bystander anymore.

He waited by the bench for one hour. It was darkening and chilly again before he gave up. He left his offering in plain sight, the roll wrapped in foil, the flask with the top screwed tight.

'Dad, can you manage to come over, soon, please.' Celia's answerphone message sounded strangely shrill. He hesitated before ringing her back. Was this a crisis that needed him to drive over the moor at night? For a second, he was tempted to let her assume he had been out all evening and had missed the message.

'Celia, is something wrong? Do you need me to drive over now, love?'

'Sorry, no, Dad, it's okay. Just would like to see you that's all. If you can. I'm off work for a couple of days. It would be nice to see you.'

'I could make tomorrow if you want.' He had a possible arrangement to meet Gabby in town, but he would ring her.

Before breakfast, he went down to the bench. It was early; frost glistened on every blade of grass; the sky was streaked with pink clouds. The flask was still there, the roll stiff and uneatable.

The drive was even slower than usual, because of a hold-up for roadworks and two lines of heavy lorries dominating the lanes. He wondered where all the cars were going and why. He had a reason to travel, but surely some of these individuals could stay at home. He had made himself laugh.

Celia was pale, drawn, distant. She made coffee; he waited. At last, she told him that the IVF had failed; there had been no successful implant. The embryos were lost. He put out his arms to her and slowly she leant into his chest. She sobbed as if her heart was pouring out of her eyes; his daughter's body shook with an intensity that shocked him. They sat together on her white sofa, while he murmured comforting nonsense into the softness of her hair.

'Come home with me. Don't stay here on your own. Let me look after you for a bit. Don't say no, love. Be looked after, I can do that.'

Wearily, wet-eyed, her face distorted by grief, she agreed. Later, as they rounded the corner to his street, he avoided looking down towards the allotment gates.

FOURTEEN

Harry appeared on the path, his pudgy face creased as he shouted to Glyn, 'I've heard you saw someone again.' Glyn was busy with a saw, shaping wood into another raised bed.

Walter was planting, the soil a tender crumb now he had worked it well, each fat seed falling into its place. He bent over each row, but had to straighten every few minutes, to let his spine recover.

He stopped now, lifted his head, shook it vigorously, giving a "no you are wrong" signal. Harry ignored him and walked past.

'That's right, isn't it? Look, I'm getting some of the others together and this time we'll catch him.'

Glyn paused. 'I don't know who told you, Harry. I did see a bloke, he left sharpish, there was no trouble.'

'There will be trouble,' Harry said. 'I'll make sure of it. He has no right to be here, on our plots. He doesn't belong. Who knows what he'll take, what he's up to.'

Walter felt panic rising. He must do something to stop this.

'There's been no damage. The pears were a professional job.'

Harry looked at him with scorn.

'I've rung round. We're doing a patrol tonight. Yours did no good, did it? We'll be on the job every night and we'll nab him. The police can take him. It's only right.'

'It's only wrong,' Walter wanted to say.

'We have to be calm,' he tried. 'There's no need to get everyone fired up. There's no harm in him.'

'You don't know that.' Harry looked sharply at him. 'Perhaps this one is a scout, seeing what we've got, what is good to get.'

The man stood there, defiantly in shorts on this chill morning and his face flushed with habitual anger. Walter thought him a cartoon man. But a dangerous one now.

'He might be one of them coming in.'

'Coming in?'

'Yeah, off the boats, illegals, coming here to take everything they can. We don't need no more foreigners. Doesn't matter, you looking like that. Goody liberals can say what they like. But they don't belong here.'

'If you mean refugees, they have a right to come and claim asylum. They are not illegal. They are fleeing from danger.'

Harry gave a short barking laugh and dismissed Walter with a wave of his hand.

'That new young lad's a definite to come, he'll be here, he's a good'un. We'll get the police down here. Get this one banged up.'

'You don't know he's done anything wrong. The police won't be interested.'

'That's what you say. I say, let's get him and then we'll see.'

Walter walked away, unable to say more, unable to act. Harry stomped off, his phone in hand. Glyn shrugged and went back to his construction.

Still holding some seeds in one palm, Walter went back to Glyn, still bent over his wooden panels.

'Did you see someone? You didn't tell me.'

'Haven't had a chance. Thought you'd emigrated.'

Walter smiled vaguely. He did not try to explain the many reasons for his absence.

'Yes, I saw our homeless intruder, the rough sleeper. Caught him, you might say.'

The beans dribbled out of Walter's hand.

'When was this? What did he look like?'

'Looked like, well, you know, looked a bit rough. Just yesterday. Can't say he was definitely a druggie, could have been, but I don't think that was it.'

'Did you speak to him?'

'Tried to, but he was off, quick as a flash when he saw me coming up the path. He was by your shed, so I took the liberty of checking the lock. It was all okay. You haven't had any damage, have you?'

Walter struggled to find the way to ask, 'Was he, do you think, was he a local?'

'No, a foreigner, definitely. Not dark, just, well, foreign. Thin, shabby-looking, unkempt, that is the word.'

'So, he went off, no trouble then?'

'There was a big fuss last week. Someone saw him or got a glimpse anyway. Harry had a hunt organised then. There was talk of getting the police, but I don't think anyone did anything about it.'

'So, what happened?'

'Nothing much in the end. Mostly noise and fuss. But everyone is cross.'

'But it's not as if anything has been taken. Not since the pears.' Walter sounded feeble to himself.

'Well. No. I don't really like the fuss, to tell the truth. Unpleasant really. But I understand it. Looks like they are going to do a night patrol now. Try to catch him. Didn't happen last time. Perhaps it will now, with Harry on the case. You tried that, a patrol, before Christmas, didn't you? Did you see anyone again?'

'No. Not a soul.' The lie was instant. Walter tried to look unconcerned. He turned away back towards his plot. But his pulse raced. What might happen to Osama if Harry and others did find him? If they got the police in, he would be taken, put into detention, put on a plane and be deported back to where he had fled from. Why does no one understand the reality? Why does no one care?

He bent slowly to pick up each speckled bean from the soil where it had fallen.

With studied casualness, he said, 'I'm a bit late with these. Usually get them in by late Feb. Anyway, they'll catch up. You don't do broad beans, do you?'

He finished his rows, following the lines of string he laid out to keep them straight, his head full of conflicting thoughts. He fumbled for his notebook in one pocket to record the date and type of bean as usual. Next to the date, he put a star and Osama's name. The pencil hovered over the page for a second. He wrote one word, "patrol", and underlined it before putting the notebook back in his jacket.

When he had carefully raked and firmed the soil, he walked back across to Glyn's plot. Pretending interest, he watched the construction process. Glyn explained each stage to him, comfortable with the observation of his skills.

'Mate, we don't need this fuss. We don't want the police, do we? Not if there's been no damage.'

Glyn lifted a hammer and said nothing. Walter paused. 'I don't like the idea of a crowd being nasty to this bloke. Is he doing any harm? Doesn't seem so. We should just leave it and see what happens.'

'Yeah, I think so too. He's a man down on his luck and we could all fall that way, eh?' Walter was cheered by Glyn's sympathy. So not everyone was hostile.

'Are you going to the jazz tonight? Looks a good line-up.'

The topic had changed. Walter went occasionally to the jazz club; it meant cheap beer and interesting music, though it was hard to get a seat unless you got there very early, and the usual crowd treated jazz as a religious matter. Casual chat turned heads and produced annoyance, shush, shush. Perhaps he would go, or say he was going, then it would be his chance to leave Celia for a couple of hours and come down to see if he could find Osama and warn him.

'My daughter's staying, so I'll see – she won't be interested. I might see you.'

As he packed up to go, he went back to say to Glyn, 'Let's hope they give up this fuss about a foreign intruder, eh?'

Glyn bent over his wooden panels without looking up to say goodbye.

FIFTEEN

He came back into the house, planning his lines to Celia, wondering how he could find Osama tonight before the so called patrol started. Could he leave him a message, or in some way divert the others? He thought of going back now and putting a warning sign of some kind behind his shed. That would be too late. Osama must be stopped from coming at all and he had no way of contacting him to do that. His mind raced helplessly. What food could he take for Osama tonight? He had two pieces of fish for supper and in his hand a bunch of parsley picked fresh for a sauce. Fish was not a suitable thing to be left on the bench and would not be good eaten cold.

'Hello, there you are at last.' Gabby was swinging her legs over the side of an armchair. There was no sign of Celia. 'I let myself in. Your back door is always open – not recommended, by the way.'

'Gabby, I wasn't expecting you.' This sounded unwelcoming. He crossed over to her and held out his arms. He kissed her warmly. 'Good to see you.'

'Hey, Stepdad, that's nice. It is good to see you too. I've come to take you out.' There was a bubble in Gabby today; he saw it rising in her eyes and heard it in her voice.

He looked around, confused now. Where was Celia? A lilac cardigan lay on the back of the sofa. Gabby followed his eyes.

'Who have you got here? A woman, is it, Walter?' She was giggling.

'That is Celia's,' he remonstrated. 'She is here at the moment, for a break, a rest. She must be upstairs, having a lie down.'

'Oh dear, is she okay? That's not like her. Is something wrong?'

Celia had been with him now for several days. This house had never been her home; he moved from there after Linda's death, encouraged by Maria before they were even lovers. Celia was a guest in his second bedroom, kept clean and neutral, only used by her. Now she slept late, ate little, went upstairs for long naps and allowed him to cook and fuss as long as he did not mention anything to do with babies, children, the future. He felt there was a loosening between them at last.

He was thinking what a suitable form of neutral and misleading words would be when Celia herself came into the room. There was a small silence. Gabby began to fuss over Celia, asking questions, being nosy. It was difficult to watch. He knew how hard this was for Celia. He needed to divert them. 'What's this about going out, Gabby? You said you had come to take me out. But, you see—'

'Dad has plans to go the jazz club, don't you?' He was

startled. He had not had a chance to tell her he might go. 'It is Friday, jazz night. You like to go, Dad, it is a favourite. You mustn't let me being here stop you.'

He realised the three of them were standing in a circle, as if fixed in a family tableau.

'Who's for a cup of tea?' He smiled at them both, turned for the kitchen.

'Me please, Dad. I'd love tea and one of your oaty biscuits, please.' His daughter crossed to the chair by the window.

Gabby said, 'I wanted to take you to this Chinese I have found in Leeds. It is great, really authentic. You would love it. And Celia, you must come too.' There was the merest hint of hesitation in her voice. Celia looked away and studied her feet. Her silence was a rudeness that Gabby could not ignore. Yet she smiled and relaxed in her chair as if she could not feel the heat of her stepsister's emotion.

He brought in a tray of tea and the biscuits on a plate.

'Sorry, Gabby. Too many choices. Jazz or not, Celia and I have a fish supper to eat, two portions only I'm afraid. So, we will have to, what do they say in the films, take a rain check.'

As she was leaving, Gabby lowered her voice theatrically, 'I have some news. Wanted to share it but it will keep.' She kissed him on both cheeks. He watched her drive off, wondering what news could keep, news that was making her smile so much.

'Dad, I thought she would never go. Do you really want to go to the jazz? It would be lovely to have a quiet evening with you. Do stay in. I feel better and there's a good film on.'

Helplessly, Walter agreed to spend the evening with his daughter, while he imagined his friend being pursued or worse. He could have said more to Harry. He could have gone down to go out with a patrol to make it alright if they found Osama. He could have stepped in to defend him then. Would he have done? He felt the weight of his own weakness heavy in his chest.

He tried to concentrate on Celia's choice of television and be glad she was warm and close. He was glad, but his mind left the room and hovered over the plots, scanning for signs, hoping for peace and finding none.

PART II

ONE

Along the dual carriageway, the May blossom foamed. The city trees had burst into showers of new green, so bright it startled. Celia had gone back to her flat and to work, refusing any making of plans. Her sadness had lifted out of the house; Walter was ashamed of how relieved he felt. He had not heard from Gabby. His life had slotted back into its usual routes. His habits sustained the days. There had been no more sightings of Osama and the patrols had stopped. People had lost interest and peace was restored to the gardens. Walter had given up leaving food and thinking about leaving food. He was relieved that the man had escaped capture. He hoped his refugee had found a refuge somewhere else. The year had turned, and he thought to himself that he had missed an opportunity, to be someone else, to do something else. He did not watch a documentary account on the TV of an Israeli attack by snipers on unarmed protesters at the Gaza border fence.

Today he was taking the car to be washed, a routine chore. Recent winds had blown blossom debris like a soft storm along the street and his car was spattered. He used a cheap place near the supermarket, quick, efficient, pleasant service. "No brushes, no scratches, hand wash only" the bright green boards proclaimed. He drove in, parked; a team of three lean, young men moved forwards, their dark faces smiling under hoods, cloths and hose in hand. It was muggy, the car suddenly uncomfortable. He got out, stood to one side, stretched his legs. The men were vigorously slicing and rubbing down the paintwork and wheel arches, a team in unison. He noticed for the first time that their clothes were damp, their feet slopping in plastic sandals. He knew he had not looked before. At the back of the parking area, there was a shaky building painted in the same violent green, a kind of temporary shed. The flimsy door shook, opened and Osama came out. His eyes caught Walter's with a flicker of recognition, but he ducked back inside, shaking his head. Walter was shocked, uncertain what he had seen, what it meant. Why did Osama not come to talk to him, acknowledge that they knew each other? He must be working here.

The three car washers smilingly indicated for him to get back in, drive around for the next part of the process. He did so, but he got out again. He walked to the back of the car. He brought out a ten-pound note and told the man who had the cash belt that he needed change. 'Where are you from?' he asked as he did so. 'Iraq, Kurdish Iraq.' The other two, finishing their thorough waxing, nodded too. The cash belt man went into the office at the side and the other two started on the next car which had driven in behind Walter. He went quickly across the tarmac to the shed.

'Osama,' he said softly. 'Come and see me tonight.'

'Many thanks, good work,' he called from the car window as he drove out, his voice loud in his ears.

*

The cool evening air held the scent of hawthorn and musk roses; his beans had sprouted; lettuces showed vivid against damp soil; the plot was alive with growth. Blackbirds and wrens fluted their songs in the trees above him, each phrase a musical call to life. Walter walked along the edge of his plot, checking his rows, noting the changes, how many new weeds needed his attention, while his mind circled around. He walked up to the next plot, along to the water tap, around Glyn's estate, crossed over to survey Sue's, looking without seeing, while his mind roamed.

He stopped by one that a new young man had taken on this year. So many plot holders underestimated the work needed to produce food. They did not realise they would have to labour like a peasant, back bent over, hands filthy and muscles sore from heaving clods of earth. They built tidy wooden raised beds and filled them with clean expensive soil in packets. But weeds were quick to take hold of any untended ground and some plots, like this one, were already defeated. Under the soil, the tendrils of bramble and chickweed roots were spreading unchecked. His own grandfather had a vegetable garden so that, in hard times, the family would have food to eat; his father, the first escapee from a mining career, grew lettuces and green beans as a homage to that childhood. Now the supermarket offered both in clean plastic. The fashion for the idea of home-grown food, organic and delicious, became the reality of bindweed that twisted its roots around tender seedlings and weather which betrayed the gardener's trust.

He was unsure if Osama would come. There was no one else around. No sign of hunters on patrol. He was unable to relax. Minutes passed, then an hour. The air grew colder, his prowling aimless. He knew he would have to leave, admit defeat.

Osama came through the open gate, entered as if he were an entitled key holder, strolling up to the bench.

'I'm glad you have come. It is good to see you, son. Sit down and let's catch up.'

Osama shook his offered hand. He looked thinner, his face was lean and darker. Walter noticed his clothes were clean, he had fashionable jeans, a different jacket. Walter's old blue one had been replaced by brown mock leather.

'Where have you been all these weeks?'

There were so many questions under his tongue, so many things unknown.

'Why don't you come up to my house? It is near. You can tell me more there. I have dinner waiting for us.'

'You are so kind. Like a father. But it is okay now. I have work, you see that. I came just to say thank you.'

Walter swallowed the words "but you are not allowed to work".

'My neighbour here, on the next plot, saw you a few weeks ago. He thought you looked, I don't know, not so good.'

'Yes, I was hoping to see you, not him.' Osama gave his slow, charming smile. 'Everything was not so okay. But now, I am on my feet again.'

'Not sleeping out then, not here?'

'No, I have a place to stay. It comes with the job.' Walter had seen the flimsy cabin on the site; was this where he slept?

'That's good. Is it good work, at the car wash?'

'It is work.' There was a hesitancy in his face as if he would say something else.

'Are your employers good?' He knew this was a ridiculous question with no answer. Why had he stumbled into this? Car washing must be cold, miserable work and that hut hardly likely to be warm or comfortable.

'Not so good, not so bad. Better than detention. I told you. I will not go again.'

Walter thought of the flashing knife and the six officers standing by as the boy ran.

'When you first saw me, Walter sir, I had been sleeping in your vegetable gardens for several days. After I ran away that time, I found it. Your garden here, what do you call it, allottement? It was my refuge.'

Walter struggled to find what he wanted to say.

'Look, Osama,' he said after a pause, 'I have a spare room in my house. You could stay at mine, for a while. And go to work from mine. Just for a while. A room of your own.'

The man shook his head, held his hand out and rose to his feet.

'You helped me. Great food. You are a cook.'

'Then come up now and eat my dinner at least. Vegetable goulash, it is spicy, not too much, good with bread or rice, your choice.'

'Not tonight. I have to go now.'

'Take my postcode, put it into your phone. It is just

round the corner. You will find it easily. Come tomorrow, at this time. What time is it? Eight o'clock – perfect.' Walter was surprised by his own insistence.

'Put my number in too. So you can ring me, any time, ring me.' He wondered why he had not thought of this before. 'Can I take yours? Oh. I don't have my phone with me, of course not. Okay, you have my number and then if you ring, I will get yours too.' He was pleased this was organised. But why had he not brought his own phone? Old fool, always forgetting to bring his phone.

Osama was leaving without a word. He turned to wave. Walter sprang to his feet.

'My daughter is a solicitor. She could help you with your case.'

'I will come tomorrow. Thank you once more.'

TWO

Osama did not come the following evening or the next. Days passed until Walter saw that the young man was not going to ring him or to come to the house. Perhaps he had to work; perhaps he was in trouble. But it was not his business. He had been thanked. He had given what he could.

He rang Celia one evening, thinking he would see how she was, and also if she would have advice for Osama.

'Let me take you out to lunch. On Saturday, this week, it is ages now since I saw you, love.'

'Dad, leave it a week or two, will you? I am so busy at the moment.'

Even at weekends, he thought ruefully. No time for your old dad, now you are feeling better. He thought of how he had rung his parents every week. He called in on them regularly. Asked questions about their day, if they needed help. Did a few odd jobs that his father could not be bothered with and which were annoying his mother. After his father died, he went to visit his mother more often. When she went into the home, he continued. After her death, he was lost for a while, without the routine of those silent moments sitting by her chair, wondering if she would remember he was there and speak.

Celia had an independent life, in another city. She did not feel responsible for him. And her generation did not have the weight of the previous one, it seemed. He must remember that. *Just as well I never asked you to investigate about Osama's case*, he thought. You would probably have said no. He wondered if she was planning another try at IVF. It seemed too difficult a subject to raise on the phone. He would have liked to ask her about the donor, the physical father who did not want to be a father, just a giver of sperm. How did it feel to create a life and take no responsibility for it? Well, there was no life, this time.

Filling his day with a walk back from the city centre, he passed a group of the hopeless boys, the lost ones who lurked on corners waiting for the drugs drop. He and Frank had long conversations about their situation, Frank tending to the view that they should all be locked up and given a very hard time. Walter thought of their missed chances, their narrow outlook, their lack of self-belief. The police ignored them, interested in the big guys. This day, one of the boys, monkish hood up, fists raised, broke away from the cluster to shout abuse across from his pavement corner to the other. Walter looked back and saw it was aimed at a figure well known for his extraordinary appearance, a fat man, Asian-looking but with long, bedraggled Rasta hair and always wearing a woolly cap of many colours. He shambled along with headphones, muttering to himself, or singing snatches of songs. The man was startled by the verbal attack flying over the air towards him, but he did not stop. He carried on going forward while the whole group of junior monks, triggered by their leader, joined in, filthy epithets, pointless and vicious. Walter stared for a moment, then he moved on too. No need to get involved, thank goodness there was no actual violence, despite the heat of those words. The insults faded behind him. Outside the Polish deli, two of the men who worked there flicked their cigarette ends onto the ground with muttered comments. The Rasta man continued on, listening to his music, humming a tune only he could hear.

Back in the house, Walter reviewed his day. His refuge, his small piece of the natural world was waiting for him, promising peace, needing attention, reminding him that his notebook had a list of tasks, necessary ones, enjoyable ones. Today, he needed people instead. He needed to talk. It was a while since Gabby's visit and mysterious news. For once he would ring her, instead of waiting for her random contacts. There was no answer; he left a message.

Later, he went down to the allotments, hoping to see Sue, hoping to have a flicker of safe excitement, telling himself that he could lose this state of mind in physical work and secret fantasy. The straw stored for strawberries would be spread out as a soft mattress; she would open her arms to him, his hands slide under her yellow coat, under the red sweater, to feel the soft firmness of her skin. He would bury his face in her warmth.

Soon there would be the first early potatoes to lift, lettuce to choose; the sweet peas would be extending up the wigwam, promising blooms to come.

THREE

'What on earth? Hey, you, back here. What do you think you are doing?'

Glyn was shouting, running up the central path, waving a hoe. Under the communal fruit trees, a figure crouched, a shape Walter knew. Osama stood up when he saw Walter running too.

He was dirty, his brown jacket gone, a shirt with a rip in one sleeve; his face was haggard and unshaven. Walter's heart thumped in alarm as he came up behind Glyn.

'Oy, you can't take our stuff. The fruit isn't even ripe. Why are you here?'

'I do not take stuff. I know the fruit is unripe.' Osama spoke slowly and clearly in his competent, accented English.

Walter stepped between them. 'I'm sure he wasn't going to take anything, were you?'

'How do you know? Look at him. He's the one I saw before. Why is he coming here if not to get something?'

'He hasn't done any harm, has he? You frightened him,

shouting like that. We don't want Harry finding out, making a fuss, do we?'

'Maybe not, old boy, but he doesn't look too good, you've got to admit.'

'He's harmless. Just down on his luck.'

Glyn gave Walter a look of surprise. 'Okay, you are happy to have some homeless foreigner, probably a refugee by the size of him, you want him coming here all the time. You talk as if you know him.'

Osama's eyes widened, a tiny grin of complicity on his lips, but he waited for Walter to react, to acknowledge their friendship.

'I just don't want everyone to get too worked up, that's all. All that nastiness,' he appealed to Glyn. 'You know how Harry gets everyone worked up. We don't need that, do we? And let's see, he needs a bit of help it seems. A bit of humane help. The best thing is for me to offer him a shower, a meal maybe, and find out what the problem is.'

'Come off it, Walter, old boy. No, we don't want the Harry types to make trouble. But you can't do that. You don't know what he might get up to.'

'He's been here before, you say, so he needs help of some kind.' The two men had been talking without a glance at their target. Now Walter turned, making a show of his action.

'Are you hungry, sir?'

'Sir?' Glyn sighed and shook his head. 'Seriously, you can't take him to your house, Walter. Come on, you can't.'

'Was that a yes? Come along with me, I won't harm you, promise, come along and let's see if we can get you cleaned up and fed.'

'Walter, don't be such a—'

'It will be alright, Glyn. Don't worry. I am no man's fool.'

Glyn watched in silent protest, leaning on his hoe, as Osama picked up his backpack and Walter led him away, down to the gate, leaving his plot untended; no gentle fantasies of Sue now needed to brighten the hour. As they reached the road, Freddie drew up in a car with two of her children leaning out of the window, their faces grinning into the blast of warm spring air. She gave him a wave, a preoccupied mother's greeting, then turned her head in surprise to look behind at the figure by his side. A little further on, he saw Sue on the opposite pavement, on her way, bustling along with her basket ready for harvest, wearing a blue gardener's apron that he especially admired. He nodded hello and kept going.

'You don't want people to know how kind you are,' Osama remarked as they rounded into his street. 'Now lots of people know.'

FOUR

'He is a liar. Your little friend. Charming, attractive no doubt if you like that kind of thing. But a liar.'

Gabby shrugged and went past him into the kitchen. 'I need biscuits, coffee, lots of coffee and a bit of a think.'

Walter stood in the hallway, unable to speak. He had been sitting at the table, waiting, pleased that she had agreed to talk to Osama after lunch. He had been full of unspoken hopes.

Osama had been here for several days now. He slept most of the first day; he showered, ate an enormous pile of rice and roasted vegetables, then he slept. Walter put him into the spare room, left towels, water, a small vase of late tulips. He tiptoed in every couple of hours. Osama slept, woke, washed, ate and went back to sleep.

Walter had not asked any questions that first day. He was glad to look after this guest and to wait. When Osama came down the stairs on day two, he sat with Walter in a patch of sunlight at the kitchen table.

'How are you now?' Walter ventured. 'Feeling better?'

'I have slept much. Thank you from my heart.'

'You've had a hard time, I can see that. Sleeping outside, sleeping on the streets or behind my shed, I can't imagine that.'

'What has my life become? I am not stupid person; I am not a bad man. Look at me, friend Walter. What do you see? Someone who has nothing.'

'You left your country for a better life, didn't you?'

'I left my country so that I would live free, I would not die in a prison forgotten. But I have not found a better life, would you say?'

'You are safe here now. Just rest, use the house, please be free in here.' It was a poor offer, Walter thought, the only one he could make.

When Gabby rang to say she had heard his answerphone message and was coming over for a chat, he had no choice but to tell her he had a visitor. He said nothing about what special kind of visitor.

When she first arrived, he took her by the arm and led her into the dining room and closed the door. Her eyebrows rose. She was laughing at him. 'Oooh, the intrigue. What is going on?'

He was brief, gave her only an outline.

'You take the proverbial you do. You have got an illegal immigrant staying with you, as a guest. Walter, Stepdad Extraordinaire, you are amazing. There is a fugitive in this house, now? What are you doing?'

Gabby sounded cheerful, encouraging almost. So he was brave. Osama was now in a steady rhythm, waking at the same early hour, waiting until Walter returned from his morning work on the plot to join him for a breakfast of bread and eggs, reading the newspaper or watching television every afternoon as if he had always lived here. He lingered over the shelves of Linda's novels as if he would like to read them. He did not pray, or if he did, Walter had not seen him. Perhaps he went into the bedroom when Walter was out. They were like housemates, calm, friendly; it was easy not to talk about what had happened, not to push for more.

So far, none of Walter's friends had called round. He had seen no plot holders; there had been no sign of Glyn or Freddie to challenge him on his early morning forays. The neighbours on the street would not have seen the stranger. But he knew the moment was coming. He knew he was doing something others might not understand. He was not sure himself what he was doing. Somehow he had started on this way, whatever it meant. Now here was lovely Gabby to help him out, shaking her head, half a grin on her face.

She agreed to stay for lunch; there was the aroma of his quiche browning nicely in the oven. A shortcrust base, baked lightly first, a filling of three eggs, half a pint of milk poured over the softened mushrooms and garlic, then a generous sprinkling of cheese. Walter took her into the living room to introduce her to his guest. The young man rose quickly to his feet and shook her hand with gentle formality.

'How nice to meet your daughter, Walter. I am delighted to make her acquaintance.'

Gabby and Walter exchanged glances. 'My stepdaughter,' he had to assert. 'I have another daughter, Celia, who,' he hesitated, 'is a solicitor.'

'Me, I'm just an estate agent,' Gabby added, brown eyes bright with hidden annoyance or equanimity, he was not sure.

Lunch had been a quiet affair, the salads delicious, he was pleased to note that the addition of chives to the potato one was good; the three of them ate appreciatively, with nods and murmurs of satisfaction around his kitchen table. When he had cleared away, refusing help from both his visitors, Gabby was ready to do as he had asked. He said to Osama that she would like to talk to him, to see if he needed help. 'I think you can talk to her. In confidence. She is good with people.' Lamely, he added, 'About your situation, if you want.'

Now he heard her words without understanding what she could possibly mean. A liar. He waited for her to explain.

'You ask him yourself. He'll tell you. He has all the paperwork. Take a look. He has lied to you.'

He breathed, tried to think. He felt as if the world was going around without him knowing what was happening. Weariness seeped into his legs. He needed to sit down.

'Gabby, you had some news. Something to tell me. What's going on with you?' He made himself focus on her. 'Come on, you came to tell me the other week and you still haven't said what it is. Good news, I hope?'

'Walter, you are a mystery.' She paused. 'Okay, not quite the way it was supposed to come out. But since you ask, I am pregnant.'

'Don't look so amazed, it is possible. I am not too old.'

'It is wonderful news.' Walter stood up to reach across the table and give her an awkward hug. 'Marvellous. How, when, who?'

'Lots of questions. In order: usual way, three months and the father is insignificant.' She beamed at him.

How can the father be of no matter? Was this another IVF, no she said it was the usual way. So? Walter thought of the simplicity of he and Linda, the sweet natural progress of their love and their child coming at last when it seemed there was no more chance of one. A pang hit him. Celia, she would find this so hard.

'We must celebrate. Yes, properly celebrate. We'll go out and then you can fill me in. All the details.' He saw her face. 'Those details you wish to share, my dear.'

He was apologetic, confused, uncertain of what to say next. 'I'm afraid, now is not the time. Please, we will arrange a date, soon, Gabby, I am happy for you.'

'I'll go, you need to talk to your man. His name isn't Osama by the way. He is called Amro.' She gathered her bag, one of those enormous soft ones women carried instead of briefcases and kissed him. 'Good luck.'

'Gabby, what shall I do?' She had gone before he could say this out loud. In the living room, Osama was staring down at the carpet. On the coffee table, there was a spread of documents, official-looking papers and a passport. Walter sat with a heavy thump and looked at them. Osama lifted his head. Walter noticed the tight curls were growing. The boy needed a haircut.

'Walter sir, please forgive. I have not told you the truth.'

'Don't call me sir.'

'Okay, but it is a matter of my respect. Now I tell you everything.'

'I am Amro... I am from Egypt.'

'Egyptian!' Walter could not stop the exclamation. All that research he had done about Palestine. Egypt. He thought of pyramids, the boy king's golden grimace under gallery lights; he remembered, as a flash in his mind, the shuffling queue for the exhibition and the girl whose hand he held; was her name Imogen? Did she have blonde hair? He could not remember; it was so long ago. He knew nothing about Egypt.

'I said I was from Palestine when the lorry opened, you know. They take you, I did not understand really, anything. I had not eaten for hours, no water even. It was cold in the lorry, very cramped under the boxes. My legs hurt, my arms, the French police, they beat us lots of times. If they catch you, they beat you. I thought the British would be more ready to accept me if I was a refugee from there. Everyone knows about the Palestinians, no?'

'Why the name change?'

'Osama is more Palestinian.'

Into the silence he added, 'It was the fear. As if they could know my name and even here in UK, they might be waiting for me. My first mistake. Stupid, stupid.'

Walter gazed at the man sitting opposite him. It seemed he did not know him at all. The strange fondness, which he had felt almost from the beginning, had grown between them over these days. *Have I been such a fool*, he thought, *tripped myself up without looking where I was going, a stupid old fool as everyone will think me. As Gabby already does, narrowing her eyes at me and leaving her news in my lap, another shock.* He was too tired to think. He did not know what to say.

'I'm going out. See you later.' He must decide what to do

now. He must act. It was time to turn his guest, the friend he had made, out again onto the streets. Celia would be furious he was harbouring someone who was here on false pretences. Everyone would blame him. He had been a fool, wanting a quiet life but taking on trouble like this. He would walk down to the plot, breathe in its peace and try to think.

FIVE

He moved his glass and indicated that they could take the empty seats on his table. He was the lone drinker taking up space. One of the four men had to pull up a stool and sit sideways, but they nodded companionably at him. The bar was crowded with Saturday afternoon drinkers already on their third. He swallowed the rest of his second pint in a few long draughts, stood and squeezed out of the corner and past noisy groups to get to the bar. Around him, people were telling tall tales, exclaiming over the miserable facts of the news, complaining about the council. He felt the beer flood his head.

The lure of the garden plot had failed him. He had turned instead into the street towards the town, as anger rose up in him. Why had he not known that this man had lied to him? Why had he been such an old fool, a silly old man? He needed to drink. He had to decide how to do it, how to tell this person to go, to leave the house and take his chances. He, Walter, had done what he could to be a friend in need, but now it must stop.

Glass in hand, he came back to his seat, but one of the men had taken it and ruefully, but not apologetically, pointed at the stool. He stood for a few seconds, ready to dispute, to claim his rights. He shrugged and drank standing by himself, his eyes roving over the crowds, looking down at those seated, getting in the way of those trying to join friends or on the search for a seat. A woman in a leather coat, open to show off her slinky red dress, gave his elbow a deliberate shove. He turned to remonstrate, gripping his glass. She winked. 'Eh, hoping for a sit down, were we? You'll have to work harder than that, love. It's everyone for himself in here. But you can come and sit on my lap if you like.' She laughed, a high tinkle of glee, and others joined in. He grimaced, moved away, felt a rush of blurriness and headed for the door. The air was fresh, making his head swim more. New drinkers arrived; he was in the doorway, in the way again. It was not a time when he might see his own friends. Frank and Janet always went out together on Saturdays and this pub was a forbidden zone.

He walked back along the high street, past the nightclubs and the restaurants, two of them now occupying what had once been banks, imposing Victorian buildings with grand entrances and inscribed dates high up on the façade. He was swaying slightly and here was another bar, one he rarely went into; it did not have real ale; it was full of young people and lager. He went in. There was one high stool unoccupied. He ordered an expensive bottle with a fancy name. It hardly mattered now.

'You can't credit it, can you? Just look around, everywhere you can see them. They have let so many in, we have to pay for them, they don't do anything but get everything. My mate has them next door. They get it free, everything new, fridges, washers, the lot all spanking new. And then they claim benefits.'

'We should turn them all out again. What does it matter to us, foreigners. Don't know any English, don't work. We need a government that'll be proper tough.'

'Don't get me started on the government. That lot. You can't trust a word. Look at what has happened. Europe, are we out? Are we...'

It was three young men. They had the swollen shoulders of those who use weights, tight against the fabric of their best shirts, their Saturday glad rags, and each held a large pitcher of lager. Walter listened, unsurprised. Also now beginning to feel his anger rising up. How could they know so little?

He swivelled on his stool and caught the eye of the loudest speaker. 'You know, the people you are talking about, the ones next door to your neighbour, they are probably Syrian families, straight from the war. The government has agreed to help them. They were in refugee camps. They had lost everything.'

They all nodded at him agreeably. 'Okay, old boy,' the loud one said, 'you say they were in the war. You don't know, you think, yes? But what has it got to do with us? Not our war, is it?' He was so pleased with this point that he had to stop to acknowledge the approval of his mates.

'They are people just like you. This is a humanitarian country.'

'They just want what we've got. Liars and cheats. Send them back, every one.'

'We don't want any more Pakis here, Pakis, whatever, scum wherever they're from.'

Walter stumbled as he climbed down off the stool. The three young men were tall enough to look down on him, their bulk a threat, despite the half grins on their faces, a tolerant "let the old man rant" look. Their viciousness was casual, unconcerned.

'Selfish, ignorant idiots,' he threw up at them. Before they could act on their amazed response, he stepped out into the street. He heard a shout behind him and quickened his pace. But they could not be bothered with him. He would become a story to pass on, to share with derision.

The bright afternoon had faded. Beneath his feet, the tarmac and the paving stones covered and suppressed the soil and all its life; the earth which he turned laboriously for his small needs was lost, hidden and forgotten, forced down and taken away. In his part of town, trees which had seen fields and the wild before them, stood marooned in concrete, massive outspread towers of leaf, presiding over acres of only air. The street names often told the story: Meadowgate End, Wood Lane, so many Groves.

He walked home arguing with himself, what he should have said, how he could have expressed the truth, the simple, humane truth. Twice he realised he must have spoken aloud as heads turned towards him.

Near the junction, there was a cluster of men, the hungry ferret-faced ones, the ones who had a shambling walk but seemed always to have a purpose as they went from one corner to the next, can in hand. They were the citizens who lived in doorways, on benches and at the back of graveyards. They did not glance at him as he passed, isolated in their own business, swaying in their huddle. They did not have the unmistakeably foreign look. They were home-grown desperados.

The house was quiet; there was no sign of his refugee. The pubs in the city had seemed a better escape today than his vegetables. Now he was hardly able to make himself proper coffee; his legs complained, and his brain was still turning round. After one cup of nasty-tasting instant coffee, he went to the foot of the stairs and called up. 'Osama, Amro, whatever you call yourself, I'm back. Do you want something?' There was silence. Considering, he went upstairs to find Osama's room empty. But his bag was still there, his shirt on a chair. He had not left, only gone out for the first time. Nosy neighbour might have seen him.

He took the last of the quiche out of the fridge and ate it without a plate, letting crumbs fall onto the floor. Inside him, a fury was intensifying. An unknown fury boiling its way into his chest. Why had he been so stupid, why had he not asked all those questions that needed asking, why did he feel this attachment to someone who was untruthful, untrustworthy? Someone who was out there now, in the city, with whoever, doing whatever. He, Walter, had no idea where the man was; he had no responsibility for him; he had no claim on him.

When he woke, it was dark; the lamp was lit; he had cramp in one leg from sitting awkwardly in the chair; and Osama was standing watching him.

'What's the time? Where have you been? What are you doing?'

'Mr Walter, please let me make you tea.'

'I don't want a teabag dunked.'

'Dun. Ked?'

Walter was forced to smile.

'I will teach you how to make proper tea. Tea in a pot, none of that wasteful nasty brown water that the girls say is tea.'

'I can use your teapot, Walter sir. I have seen you do it.'

'No, it's alright, lad. I need to go to bed. Let's talk in the morning. You can tell me tomorrow.'

He stretched his legs, nodded to his guest and went upstairs to find a heavy, uncomfortable sleep.

SIX

'So, you are not an asylum seeker.' He had raised his voice and was ashamed. 'You are what they call an economic migrant. You came here for a better life. More money, is that it?'

They had eaten a silent breakfast, a Sunday morning treat of croissants, Walter's favourite way of marking the weekend. He knew Osama was waiting for him to start, but any words were hard to say. He took the coffee cups to the sink to be rinsed, then turned sharply and began.

Osama stood up so they were facing each other across the kitchen floor. Sunshine gleamed on the tiles.

'I am Egyptian. My name is Amro. I have a passport to prove it, here, you can see.' Osama had brought a blue cardboard file downstairs. It had been waiting on the side for this conversation to begin.

'Look. This is the truth. The truth is better. I am glad to tell you.' The man faced Walter with pride. 'I have my degree certificates, my CV, a reference from my university. Let me show you. I was a maths lecturer.'

'I don't understand.' Walter had never asked questions about Osama's education and his previous working life. A lecturer, a maths teacher.

'I ran away. My parents told me to go. The police were looking for me. There is no justice in my country.'

'So, you are a criminal? You are a fugitive.'

'Please, dear sir, I am a refugee. I was in the spring protests, you know I think about them, on the streets. They pick you out from photos and come for you in the night.'

Walter found he still had a cup in one hand. He put it down. The smell of coffee lingered. He had been on protests as a young man and even more recently. A group of fellow students got the night bus down to London to go to the second Vietnam march. He remembered it as one of the highlights of those days; it was exciting, purposeful, a communion of minds and voices, hope and anger raised into the sky. To be in London in the city centre was in itself an adventure for a boy from the north. The ranks of policemen lining the way had been a shared enemy, their eyes locked on you as if you were a real threat. A peaceful day in fact, a loud, protesting, peaceful crowd. A few years ago, he went with Frank and Gerry to march against the Iraq war, a huge turnout again on the city streets which proved fruitless.

'You were a Muslim Brotherhood supporter.' He had read a little about the Arab uprisings. This man, Amro, was a Muslim and this party had been part of the trouble there, he was sure.

'No, I was not.'

Seeing Walter's confusion, he said, 'It is very complicated. My country is a terrible place.'

'So why were you protesting?'

'I was at the university. I was lecturer there. My students were angry, very full of anger about the government. I joined them. We wanted democracy. We wanted to be free.' He laughed, a harsh sound.

'You did get rid of the government though?' Walter knew that had happened.

'It was so glad, all of us at the beginning. So much force, so much joy.'

He was quiet for several minutes.

'The army became the police. They fought us. And then, you know, it was a matter of who you can trust. Trust in the authorities we never had. Then we did not have trust in others. Who were you loyal to? Who did you belong to? These are what you find as the truth. Nothing is safe. You do not know who will betray you. If the army or the police get you, they will kill you, torture you first, leave you to rot, no one will see you again.'

How proud Walter had been to be one of those who joined in protests, the type of conscientious person who rallied to the right cause. And all without effect. Or danger.

'If they knew anything, the officers at the port, the Home Office people, if they knew anything at all, they would know I am not Palestinian.' He laughed again. 'I don't look like a man from Palestine. I speak Egyptian Arabic. It is different.' His shrug expressed the stupidity and ignorance of those in authority.

'You do not like Arabs. Maybe not you, Walter, sorry, but the English. We are all the same to you.' Walter said nothing.

'I could have had a life these last five years, nearly six now, yes,' seeing Walter's expression, 'a life in my own country, maybe be married, have children.'

'How old are you?'

'Forty-two.' Walter had thought him a boy, maybe a young thirty at the most.

'You have been here five, six years?'

'Yes, I look young, I know.' This with a flash of vanity, the handsome man aware of his impact.

'I had to come here. My family, everyone told me, they will come for you, go now. It is a terrible thing. I did not go home after work that day, when I got the phone call. So, I have had six years wasted, hoping, not able to work, not as I should, no money, nothing, no life for years. I only want to belong. I do not belong here. I do not even belong back there. Not anymore.'

Walter closed his eyes. An image came to him. A dark space, light seeping in. Noise, voices, official shouts. Fear, cold. A stumbling through. The words all wrong.

He opened his eyes.

'I have been trying to make my case. When it was refused, I have been to the Palestinian embassy in London to get papers – not a proper embassy, they don't have. I have had a solicitor who has been good. A friend. But it is hopeless.'

'Hopeless because you lied. You are not Palestinian. How could they say you were, how could they give you papers?' His voice was louder again. It was so quiet in the room. He felt the weariness along his chest and down into his legs. 'Why now, Osama, sorry whatever your name is, Amro? Is that right? Why are you saying this now? Why are you telling the truth now, to me? If truth is what it is.'

'Because your daughter, your stepdaughter, Gabriella is sharp; she saw that I stop for a moment, am not sure. And you are my friend.'

He is a friend. The confusion Walter was feeling shifted inside him. My friend.

'I am tired. The truth is better. At least I am who I am.'

'You were working at that car wash. So, you were working illegally?'

'I am refused asylum. No work. No benefits. I cannot work legally. But I have to live. What does your government think we will do? What can we do?'

'Why didn't you say hello that day? Where have you been? What about your job?'

'Someone told on me. Some friend, haha, said something, made a phone call, I don't know. That job was no good anyway.' He laughed, his hard, dry laugh. 'As if it was that job I wanted. They are crooks those people; they don't pay what they promise. You owe them money from the beginning. But someone wanted my job. That is how low I sink.'

'You have worked in other places? Lived in other places. You have not always been homeless?'

'I had a girlfriend.' There was a fierce light in Amro's eyes.

'The Polish lady?'

'Yes. A lovely lady. Now that is over.'

'You did live with her. Yes?' Amro nodded, his head lowered. Walter changed the subject back. 'So what happened at the car wash?'

'A man I know, who knows me, he wanted to work there. So, he reported me. They came, the officers. It is like being arrested. A criminal.'

'Did you tell them you are not Palestinian?'

'I told them nothing.'

Walter could say nothing, hearing the man's despair, knowing his own ignorance.

'But they didn't send you to a detention centre again. Why not?'

'Now I have to report to the Home Office – in Leeds. Every two weeks. I have been one time already. So, I cannot work any longer. They may take me again to the detention. If they wish. If they decide. But no, I did not tell them who I am. Only you and Gabriella know.'

Silence grew in the room as they sat opposite each other, both heads bowed, eyes unseeing.

'Where is your girlfriend now? Won't she help you?'

'She is not my girlfriend now. We are finished. She does not want me. She wants a man who can work, pay his share. Do you want me to go?' Osama, it was impossible to think of his other name, rose out of the chair. 'I can go. I will find somewhere. It is okay.'

'No, sit down. Let me think. Let me rest.' He was so tired. He would force himself to go out and plant the last of the leeks. He would look for Linda under the apple trees and try to think.

SEVEN

The fresh green of spring had softened; once tender shoots were now standing firm; the runner bean seedlings he had been nurturing on the kitchen windowsill were beginning to wave their tendrils, ready for planting out. He would spend today with the satisfaction of growth and peace. The Home Office reporting was a day of painful tension and anxiety which he could manage on his plot, staying out until it was nearly time for the man to return. If he had his hands in the earth, his mind could swerve away from what might be happening, what might have happened. The threat that Amro would be detained rose up each time but was not spoken. The fear was a new presence in his house. He had looked up detention centres again one night, restless before bed, sitting with a screen to pass the hour as if it was a casual interest. The stories were chilling.

Tidying the rooms as he always did before he went out, then picking up his garden notebook to take with him, he was startled out of reverie by Amro appearing in front of him.

'Walter sir, can I cook for you tonight?'

'No need, I have a meal planned.'

'No need but I would like to, sir.'

'Less of the sir, please. And sorry to be direct, but what will you use for the ingredients? And don't you have to go to Leeds today?'

He was surprised by the force of his own words. But the man had no money, no work of course; he was not allowed to work, and it was his day to report to the Home Office. Walter had already put out cash for the bus fare.

'I am sorry. I cannot buy. I can only cook. And Leeds market is very cheap, I think. I can buy cheap vegetables, lots for a little.' He smiled, but his charm was uncertain.

Walter nodded briskly. 'Okay, whatever you like. See what you can get for the money in the house tin. By the kettle. There should be enough. And you should get change.' He was not sure how much was in the tin. This was the first time he had let his guest shop, take money, cook. *A line has been crossed today*, he thought. His own careful habits, planning ahead, making sure he could see the shape of a day, a week, know how his time would fill and pass, now there was a break. The days had passed quietly since he had discovered the truth of Amro's story. It was difficult to remember to use the new name. There were so many questions unanswered, hanging between them. But he let the days slip past with the new rhythm the two of them had created. It was peaceful, easy. He liked having another person in the house, another man. Without scenes, demands, anxious conversations to be negotiated.

Amro asked him every day what was for dinner, timidly

at first as if he had no right to know. Once he realised how Walter planned his weekly meals, took time to consider the menu, he joined in.

'You must let me cook, my food, one day, yes?' His eyes sparkled with a new enthusiasm.

Walter found him over a recipe book, the old, much used one which was Linda's favourite.

'That's typical English cooking, traditional. More than me these days. Lots of meat. Not the food you like anyway.'

'I like this country. I like your cooking, Walter. So maybe I can learn this cooking. Not the meat maybe. There is lots of rice, pasta in this book. Of course. Pasta, pasta, everywhere I see pasta in this town.'

'It is cheap and filling, that's why. You can go out for dinner and not pay too much, and the restaurants can still make money,' Walter said. 'Do you like pasta?'

'Of course. I shall cook you pasta my way.'

'Yes please.' Walter's interest in what he ate had returned and now he could share it with this man. Amro wanted to learn. So did he.

Once a day, Amro went out for a walk. Walter suspected he was going to see people he knew, but he did not ask. The man was always back in the house for a meal in the early evening. He asked about the ingredients, commented on the flavour. He was an enjoyable companion at the table. No more meals on Walter's knee. After they had eaten and cleared away, Amro would watch the TV programme Walter chose, rise immediately when the news came on as if he could not bear it, smile politely and say goodnight. Walter went out as usual to meet his friends in the pub without telling anyone who he was living with. He spent a long Sunday afternoon with Frank discussing the political farce unfolding at national level without a word of Amro's predicament. Gabby had been silent too; there were no phone calls for two weeks from daughter or stepdaughter, only one text from Celia saying little.

This calm hit the fortnightly blockade of the visit to the Home Office. The threat of detention, of a violent change and of deportation for Amro, hung in Walter's mind and in the very air of the house. He could ignore it until the morning of the visit when he woke, aware immediately of the date. As the hour for him to set off came near, Amro was very quiet, composed but tense; he only nodded his appreciation of the bus fare and Walter's implicit support. There was the unspoken, but loud, reality, perhaps this time he would not come back. Today, his third time going to report, he had made this suggestion about cooking, shopping in the market; he had brought this new idea into the house.

'Dad, are you going to be in later? Thought I would pop over. I've a day off and haven't seen you for ages.' Her voice was high as if she was excited.

'Celia, what time, love?' He could not tell her anything on the phone. Gabby might have passed on the "your father is living with an illegal immigrant" story, but he knew their communication was limited to photos on Facebook and other social media of a type which he could not fathom.

He had time to do part at least of his planned day, the planting, a little watering, but now he must think about food. Amro would be back by early afternoon. Celia would stay for dinner too if it was early enough. She needed to get back for work the next day. She would meet his visitor. He would have them both in the house. Why was she coming now? He had tried to see her more than once, volunteered to drive over, now she was just turning up as if he has no life of his own. She could have given him notice.

He would think about the problem while on his plot. He would have to explain the whole thing to her. He would make her understand that Amro needed help. Deserved his help. And he had to be sure for himself too. Walter did not want to wonder if his trust was unshakeable, if he was making another kind of mistake.

EIGHT

'Sorry I'm so late, Dad. I left a bit after I meant to, true, sorry, but the traffic was dreadful. Queuing all the way from Huddersfield – just twenty miles an hour if it moved at all. No reason, the roadworks, of course, as always, but then a slowdown and no explanation.'

From the kitchen there was a scent of cooking, an aroma of something spicy and unrecognisable. The radio was playing different music from a station Walter did not recognise.

'I was going back tonight but I don't think I can face that again today – is it alright if I sleep? I can ring in and say I am working from home on a case – I could stay here and actually work on a case.' She laughed as she stretched long slender legs out along the sofa. For work, her outfits were always formal, narrow black skirts, white shirts tucked in. Today he saw she was in tight jeans and a floaty blouse with a leaf print in sugar almond colours. She looked softer, freer, her hair less sleek. He shrugged in what he hoped was an amused fashion while his mind raced.

'I'll have to go upstairs though, before that tea. I've been in the car for hours, honestly, I should have been here two hours ago.'

He went into the kitchen. Amro grinned at him, steam rising from more than one pot. The surfaces Walter cleared, tidied, wiped every day were cluttered with bowls and packets, jars and vegetable peelings in little piles. Walter stifled his reaction.

'Your daughter has arrived? I will come and meet her in just a minute. I will finish this stage.'

Walter carried three cups of tea in. Celia was standing in the centre of the room. She gave him a puzzled look.

'Dad, there is someone in my room. You have a guest. You didn't tell me.'

Behind him, Amro appeared, smiling, holding out his hand. He was wearing an old apron of Walter's around his waist and a white shirt which made his pale olive skin shine darkly.

'I am so delighted. You are the dear daughter. Very pleased to meet you. How are you?'

Celia shook the offered hand, smiled uncertainly back.

'Celia, this is Amro. He is staying here at the moment. And he is cooking our meal. Would you like a sandwich first if you are very hungry? I have ginger cake too. But sometimes you don't eat cake? I think he plans to have it ready early – is that right?'

'Yes, Sir Walter, another half of an hour and it will be on the table. Thank you for the tea. Please excuse me, I must cook.'

'What's this? Sir Walter. Dad, I don't understand.'

'It's not Sir Walter, he just, I asked him not to call me sir, to use my name, but he uses sir to be respectful – it is funny, he keeps doing it, we laugh about it.'

Celia gazed at him. 'We laugh about it? Why is he here? Have you taken a lodger?'

'Sort of. Yes, that's it. He is my lodger. For a while.'

'So, he's paying you rent then; you have let my room to a lodger. My room. Do you need the money?'

'Celia, love, strictly speaking, it is not your room. There is still the box room for you to stay in. Please do stay tonight, any time, it's fine, this is a temporary situation.'

'Oh, I see. Your only daughter doesn't have a room in your house. You can take in a stranger, a foreigner, without a word to me.'

'Please don't let's fall out. Please, I can tell you all about it once we have eaten. Amro has gone to a lot of trouble with this meal.'

After Linda died, and Marie started taking him out, he moved from the family house in Sandal to this smaller one near town, with a manageable garden and no memories of death in the bedroom. Marie and Gabriella had lived here; Celia had always been a visitor.

'Please come. Dinner is ready. Dear daughter, please sit here. Sir is always at the head.'

Thank goodness, Amro seemed unaware of the tension they brought into the kitchen with them. Celia's pale face was flushed pink. He was sure he looked upset. If Amro noticed, he played the host, unruffled.

The table was set with a basket of flatbreads, small bowls of aubergine dip, tomato and cucumber salad, hummus. Walter recognised the blue pottery Linda had collected on holidays in Greece, long consigned to the back of the cupboard. In the middle, there was his carving plate, turned into a platter. It looked like onions, rice, a kind of small pasta Walter did not know, a surprising mixture heaped in the centre, steaming gently.

'This is koshari. It is eaten a favourite in Egypt. I do not think I can do it like my mother. But I try. I hope you like it. If you do, I can give you the recipe, Walter sir.'

He began offering the bowls, spooning food onto their plates. Celia was stiff, quiet, polite, accepting the food without comment. Walter saw she was using the manners of habit, but he could feel the chill spreading from her.

'This looks wonderful. A feast. I think you had better tell us all about it, Osama, Amro, sorry. What have we got here?' He knew he was making it worse. And using the other name, what a stupid mistake.

Smiling, calm, in charge, the cook explained the dish. Koshari: green lentils, rice, vermicelli which Amro called small pasta, fried onions, cooked separately, now piled high together.

'Please let me help you. Here, do try it. It is delicious.'

Amro seemed happy. The word which came into Walter's mind was vivacious. He was talkative, as charming as he could be, describing each dish. He held out the basket piled with warm flatbreads.

'I found these in the stall in the market. Have you seen that stall, Celia? Do you know it? In the corner?' He spoke excitedly. 'It is great. Food from the Middle East. My part of the world.' He leant over, offering the breads with a smile.

'They look like the ones my mother buys from our baker every day. These are good. Please try. And it is all cheap, Walter. Change is in the tin.'

There was little conversation once they began eating; they all ate with relish, even Celia. The meal passed. The unexpected mixture was good. But Walter was waiting for the moment when they could sit back, make sounds of satisfaction so he could stand up with determination to clear the table.

'Sir Walter.' He winced, unable to glance at Celia. 'Let me do that. I am the chef today and I clear up. I wash dishes. Please sit with your dear daughter.'

Dismissed, they had to retreat to the sitting room, with cups of coffee in the tiny espresso cups which he never used, a relic of Marie's presence in his life, that Amro had found and filled with a thick, sweet coffee.

The room grew heavy with the unspoken. He felt the wall behind him as listening ears despite the clatter of Amro washing up. He must say something, explain, let her talk. But he was silent while she sat with her head bent over the coffee. At last, she said, 'So now the illegal is in our house. What's his name? What did you call him?' Walter shook his head, tried to start.

'You are letting him have everything, cook, everything it seems. Did you buy those ingredients? Did you give him money? Do you give him money?'

Walter wanted to say, 'It is none of your business; it is my house and what I do here is for me to decide. Why are you accusing me? What are you accusing me of, exactly?' He swallowed, paused, said as gently as he could, 'Celia, you know something of this man's story. I have learnt more since Christmas, and I am happy to help him as far as I can.'

Her eyes were sharp, blue, unrelenting.

'So how long is this going to go on? You can't help him really, can you, if his claim has failed? He'll have to go back. He'll be detained. You'll have the immigration police here, in this house. And why did he mention Egypt? What's the plan, Dad? What next?'

She pushed her cup away, knocking the saucer. 'Have you told Gabriella about all this? You two are always thick as thieves. Does she know about this secret lodger?'

He stumbled over the words. 'He is not a secret, Celia.'

'So, you have told Gabby, is that it? Are you going to adopt him? You got yourself an extra daughter – is it a son you want now?'

He got to his feet. 'That's absurd. And insulting. I am going to see if he does need any help in the kitchen and then go out for a walk.'

He was ashamed to leave her there, to go past Amro without speaking, out into the evening, the sky still a blue bowl, now hazy at the edges. He was ashamed to wonder what Amro would think of her, what judgement he would make of this cold person, so unsympathetic, so harsh.

He could not leave them both in his house, his daughter furious, ready to act as prosecutor, while Amro played the helpful guest, unsuspecting. He would walk around the block, up along by the site of the old hospital and quickly back.

His phone bleeped. There was a text from Celia – "Going home now. Speak soon".

NINE

The kitchen was quiet, clean. All the debris of the meal cleared away. There was no sign of his house guest. Walter sat heavily in a chair, closed his eyes and let his mind go blank. He was startled by Amro tiptoeing past. 'Sorry, I did not want to wake you.'

'Not sleeping, lad. Just thinking.'

'I am going out now. Is there anything I can do for you?'

Walter hesitated. 'Did you see my daughter before she left?'

Amro was still, his face solemn. 'She was in a hurry. I think she needs to go to work in the morning. She has a long drive, yes?'

Walter understood that he was repeating what Celia had said to him. So, she had been polite, had made excuses. Had Amro heard the raised voices, her furious accusations?

'I think you are upset?'

For a second, Walter was ready to deny this. He had no intention of opening up to this man. Family business was for family, his own anger with Celia inexpressible, hot in his chest.

Amro offered a smile. 'You have one daughter and one stepdaughter. You are lucky man.'

'They are jealous of each other. Not so lucky.'

'But that is family, no? Always jealous. Two girls, each want you to love them most. But you love this one, the first one, I think.'

'Of course. She is my daughter. Gabby is a blessing, an extra. But Celia, I find it difficult to get close to her now. Her mother died. She was young, while she was still at university.'

Amro was sitting opposite him now, leaning forwards, tilted towards him. 'That is hard.'

Walter wanted to stop. He had said enough. Sympathy at this moment was uncomfortable. He was not sure what he was feeling, why he wanted both to sleep and to cry.

'Does she talk to you?'

Walter was silent. Your children talk to you the way they want to, say only what they think you need to hear. But he had been close enough to Celia. She did confide in him about the IVF, his and her secret, she said. He had looked after her as much as he could. That was all you could expect. He did not deserve to be treated like this. Why was she so cold, so harsh?

'She is sad, I think. My mother is sad because of my brother dying, such a long time ago, but she still weeps.'

'I will make some tea.' Walter went into the kitchen, but instead of the kettle, he picked up a bottle of wine from the rack. Since Amro had been here, he had not drunk in the house, showing respect to the man's religion. Nonetheless he took two glasses, placed them on the side table and offered the bottle. Amro nodded. The two men drank together, quietly sipping the deep red liquid as the light faded. The confusion of Walter's feelings subsided. He relaxed his shoulders as the wine seeped into him.

'Can I ask you something? Is it not against your faith to drink?'

Amro nodded. 'But we always need to break the rules.' This with a shrug and a grin. 'Only on special times.'

'Special occasions you mean. Is this one then?' He was moved.

'The first time we sit like this, two men. And you have a bad day.' This was said gently, firmly and confidently. Walter stared. He thought of Linda watching him, listening from somewhere unknown. Their daughter, in this house, shouting at him.

'Why is she so cross? That's what I don't understand. Why is she so cold?'

'Sadness is deep. She hurts.'

They lapsed into silence again. The level in the wine bottle dropped. It was time to turn on the lamps, watch the news, prepare for the end of the day. As he locked the back door, feeling his feet uncertain for a moment, Walter remembered that Amro had intended to go out. He had kept him here from whatever he had planned. He must apologise, though it also seemed to him an unnecessary courtesy now. The companionship of these hours had warmed him like the wine.

'Sir, thank you for this time. I will not be drinking again. I am drunk.' Amro laughed behind him. Walter turned and

Amro caught his shoulders. 'So goodnight. In my country, we say it like this.' He gave him a swift, light kiss on both cheeks. 'Sleep well.'

Walter looked at the back of his tall frame as he left the room.

'Goodnight, my friend.'

TEN

He woke early to another bright day, the light streaming in around the curtains, promising heat. A day for gardening, for planting and action. He lay immobile, listening out for Amro, wondering if he could go to Manchester, if he should ring Celia early, if he wanted to have the day to himself. No answer came. In the next room, he heard movement and sounds like groaning. When he had washed and was considering breakfast, Amro appeared, red eyed and with an unusual, bedraggled air.

'Drink is very bad. A very bad thing for me. Never again.' He gave a dramatic groan which made Walter laugh.

He offered tea. 'Was that the first time?'

'My girlfriend, she drinks wine and sometimes beer and those small ones, shots? But it has been a long time. And for me, only on special times – special occasions, you say.'

'Oh dear. You overdid it. Me too. Once half a bottle was no bother – I'm getting old. Drink the tea – have sugar in it. That might help.'

'Sir, can I make coffee?'

Walter offered his old cafetiere which Amro took and placed at the side of the kettle.

'Can I show you how we make coffee at home?'

Walter watched as he boiled water and grounds in a small saucepan, the resulting mixture thick. Amro put sugar in each of the two small cups, found in the back of the cupboard. Walter was going to protest that he did not take sugar, but he was quiet.

He began to collect eggs and bread for toast. Without asking, he fried the eggs in olive oil and served them both a plateful, the yolks shiny gold and the toast sticky with butter.

As they sat over the crumbs, Walter asked him about the mosque. Where did he go? Who did he know who was a Muslim too? The local community went to mosques in houses, he knew that. He had never noticed minarets here as in other cities, where the mosques were grand decorative buildings standing proudly above the skyline. He could only tell which was a mosque if he happened to see a congregation of men streaming into a terraced house in one of the streets nearby on Fridays. The cathedral dominated the shopping areas, unmissable in its stone bulk, spire stretching upwards over everyone's heads. He listened to Amro explaining that there were different sections, types in the faith, a Kurdish Group, an African group, and that he himself went to pray at the one where there were many Arabic speakers. *Fridays*, Walter thought, *that's where he goes every Friday morning.*

'There are minarets. Don't you see them? By the old station, not the new one, that old place, around the corner – look up, you will see it.'

Walter thought how he never looked up. His own eyes

were always cast down, being careful to watch his feet on uneven pavements or only lifted high enough to spot which pedestrians to avoid.

'So, you drink sometimes. Meat? What about meat?'

'No. I could not. Not if it is not halal. Only, you know, my family, what we all believe, it is too far.'

Walter nodded. 'We're all products of our upbringing.'

'There are halal butchers in your town. There is one at the back of the paper shop, on the corner.'

Walter made more tea. He had never considered that there might be Islamic butchers here in his town. He had not thought of trying to buy Osama the kind of meat he would like. Perhaps now he would. There was so much he had not done, had not thought of doing.

'Tell me about your family. Your parents, are they still alive?'

'They are old, Walter. Old not like you, they are old and sick. I have a photo of my mother. Wait, I will get it for you.'

From his wallet, a folded and faded photograph. She looked severe, her head wrapped in dark cloth, her face hawkish and still. Her eyes were bright and met the camera directly.

'See, she is only young there, more than ten years ago this was taken. Now her health is not so good.'

'Can you get through to them on the phone?'

'Yes, I text, ring, when I have credit. My cousin too, he is still there, tells me how they are, what happens.'

'Where do they live?'

Amro began to describe the village outside Alexandria which he had once called home.

'It is very different there from the city. My mother had little education, but my parents wanted me and my brothers to do well in the world. To get a good education, to leave for work if we had to. My sisters, they only had some school, you know, they were prepared for marriage. Even my oldest sister who was a rebel until she was sixteen. Then she gave up, I think. Accepted her fate.'

As he talked, Walter saw images of high grasses in fields, donkeys with loads in baskets, women draped in black, dusty paths and the wide river, oars through the slow water. He saw it like a Thomas Hardy novel, a country life long lost but dreamed of, held fast in the mind. He had read those novels and loved those stories when he was young, in his first forays into literature. But Amro told him how he had longed to get away from a harsh and narrow life, to university in the city, then work in the university after graduation. He had chosen an urban life. A life, Walter thought, where concrete and tarmacadam had crept forwards to cover the earth as everywhere.

'But now, Walter, I think perhaps it is not such a bad way to live. I wanted to escape that life so much. The city was modern, like here you know, big, so much to do. And I always thought England was the place I could go to one day, as a lecturer, maybe a professor in one of your grand old universities. I would be respected as an expert in my field.' Amro shook his head vigorously as if to shake the words out.

The two men sat at the kitchen table.

'So now I have nostalgia, is that what you say? Is that the word? A longing for home.'

The day was going to be very warm; sunshine glanced

off the tiles and moved across the floor. The kitchen smelt faintly of oil. It was quiet outside; the neighbours were at work, except for the nosy one and she had gone shopping. Walter wanted to ask questions, to ask about what had happened to him, why and how he had escaped, if escape was the right word, how had he got here to this country. It did not seem right to ask anything. Despite all his research, he knew too little, felt his ignorance as a hard fact, a block to understanding. He could only accept what he was offered. Amro was wistful; his voice had dropped; he shuffled the mugs back and forth on the tabletop as the story went on.

'Did you have a girlfriend there, at home, in the city?' Walter asked.

'No, not one. Well, more than one.' Amro grinned. So, the player, the handsome man with lots of love interests and no commitment. Walter had been exactly the opposite; *I fell in love with Linda and that was that. Now I could play the field, but the gate is closed. No one notices an old man. Sue must think I am a dear old fool, nothing more.*

Amro lifted his head and said, 'Tell me about your daughter.' Walter was silent for a few minutes. 'It is not necessary. It is okay if you do not want to say.'

'I don't know. I am so angry with her about yesterday.'

He did not want to say that he knew little of her life, that this dear child was a distant star. For a few days after the IVF failure, she had been here in the house, while she needed his care. They had not talked much – she had not confided in him – but he felt her close. He understood she was in pain and was pleased that he could protect her as when she was young.

Amro said how attractive she was. 'Such a lovely young lady. Clever too. She is lawyer, you say.'

'She stayed in the city after she got her degree, to study the law. It is a long process for those qualifications. Like you, she wanted to be somewhere bigger.'

'This is not a village,' he laughed.

'No, not like your village. But it is a small place, it hasn't all those, all the excitements of a big city like Manchester. And her mother had died. Linda died in our bedroom. She was ill for months, came home at the end from the hospital. I wanted her with me, with us.'

'She was beautiful, I think, like your daughter.'

In the end he could barely look at her. He held her very gently in his arms, stroked her face, took her shrunken hand in his, but it was so hard to open your eyes and see the whole of her, her lovely whole ruined by the disease. He was careful to keep those memories in a separate place. She came to him now fresh, his wraith, as a young woman. If she had lived, she would be an old woman, marked by age which is crueller to women than men. This he could not see. He was sure she would not have become the solid columns he saw of other women, their outlines rubbed out and filled in. His Linda would still be the same with curves and softness. If her fair hair had begun to fade into silver, it would still be beautiful, still gleam in the firelight.

'They were alike in some ways. Celia is... she is taller.'

'I think it is a pity she does not have children, your Celia. She does have a boyfriend? Do you hope she will have children one day?'

'She's a career woman. She works hard as a solicitor. There

have been boyfriends, but no one for long. It's work she cares about.' This direct fabrication sounded loud to his own ears.

'Linda was, how you say, a housewife?'

'She would never have accepted that term, lad. She was a feminist, they all were then, campaigning for equality. The whole shebang. Put the toilet seat down. You wouldn't know about that, would you?' seeing the wrinkle on Amro's face. 'But she didn't have a degree, so she worked in the local government, like me. That's where we met. Not a professional job and she wasn't promoted – became ill just when she might have been able to go further, do less for Celia, you see. She died too young.'

'You married again?'

'Marie. You could say she married me. Set out to get me, and I was lucky she did. She was a good person, fun too. But it didn't last. Linda was the love of my life, and you can't have that twice.'

'You miss her too. You and Celia, you are both sad.'

'What about your love life, son? Eh, what about that woman you lived with. Lovely you said.'

'She was lovely. It was good. But when I was refused a second time, she did not want a man who could not work, had no rights. She would not take me to meet the rest of her family. She could not understand my situation. I was no use to her.'

'Did you tell her your story was a lie? That you were not from Palestine? That was why you could not get the right papers to prove you were?'

Amro shrugged. 'No, I could not. I was no use to her.'

He and Walter exchanged the glances of two conspirators, two men sharing the reality of women in their lives.

*

Frank rubbed his hand up and over his face, put down his empty glass and fixed him with a long, assessing look.

'What's going on here, my old mate?'

The pub was thinning out after the early evening rush of workers. Their table had held three other drinkers but now they had its smeared surface and the beery air of this corner to themselves. It was difficult to know what to say first, if to say anything. The chat over two pints had been easy, comfortable; the usual topics had been covered: music, television, setting the date for their summer walk. Frank was not a sensitive man. He did not notice many things in his friends' faces. Or if he did, he was quiet about it. Walter did not expect to be quizzed. Yet here was his question and the searching into his eyes. Frank had noticed his preoccupation, that his mind had wandered off along different paths. He could shrug this off. It was so confusing to explain. A Muslim asylum seeker who had lied to the authorities about his identity; a stepdaughter who was pregnant by who knows who; a darling daughter who he was not speaking to. He sighed heavily enough to signal that he could not start. The question was closed. Frank shook his head.

'Okay. Let me know when you have cheered up. Another one?'

PART III

ONE

The hot weather continued. Temperatures were recorded that were the highest for decades. Walter kept a careful record. The public mood changed from excited to complaining. Everyone everywhere was in a sweat. The watering on his patch was a new kind of labour as the use of hosepipes had now been banned. Walter had to walk up to the allotment tap, fill his heavy metal can and walk back again, then again and again. One can hardly wet the thirsty soil. His early mornings were now not an indulgence but a necessity.

The sun had brought growth; his long, straight rows were bursting with green, lettuces bolting upwards, radishes showing pink tops. French bean plants curled skywards and flowered too soon. He could come home each day with something green to cook and eat in his basket. He had lifted tiny early potatoes to be eaten with salt. Soon the pods of broad beans would fatten, and he could pick out the beans from the furry insides. The fruit bushes would be drooping with berries before too long.

Sue stopped to ask his advice about her plot.

'Look at my lettuces now. What have I done wrong?'

Instead of his rows carefully planted with the use of a stick and twine, she had stuck her seeds in by eye, leaving the ground marked in wiggling lines and wasteful curves. He did not say this to her. Order was important to him, but not to others perhaps. He could see she had watered too little and then too much, a common mistake which meant her lettuces had flopped and her spinach was not germinating.

But he was kind, offered some tips. She was wearing shorts that held the small barrels of her thighs in a firm grasp. Her top lip was faintly beaded. It was so hot that day. His mind stalled.

One morning, when the heat had still to rise, and his back had not yet started to ache, he dug over her compost heap, turning out perennial weeds which needed to be burnt, throwing aside sticks she had carelessly thrown in, relayering the whole thing with chopped green stuff, covering it properly with a frayed piece of rug from behind the shed. She rushed down when she found it, trotting along the path with a flushed happy face and a wide smile. He had to hide his embarrassed delight when she threw exuberant arms around him.

'You are such a dear.' He nearly suggested they could go for a cold drink somewhere. But the words stayed in his throat.

The work of planting, weeding, watering, filled his mind as well as his muscles. It was an escape from worry and confusion to rub the earth through his hands and smell the rich aromas of summer. He watched the bushes, hoping to see the fox. There would be cubs in a burrow at the wild edges which might come out to play if he was lucky. Linda's wraith was absent. He could not feel her presence these days.

Gabby came to see him one Saturday, swinging up the allotment path with her bouncy stride. 'Hello, Grandad,' she joked. He was startled. 'How's you?' she rattled on. 'I knew I would find you here. Gosh, it is too hot today for all this work. Can I sit on the bench? At least it's in the shade. I've brought lemonade. It's still cold. It's not as good as your homemade, but it is a superior make.'

They drank the icy fizz sitting companionably side by side. She pretended to be interested in his vegetables, but it was a cursory attention. He wanted to stare at her outline. She did not look obviously different, but her clothes had a flowing shape, and her cheeks were rounder. Her arms next to his were softly fleshy. She was wearing a yellow shift, against which the olive tone in her skin glowed. The fabric moved around her as she talked, so that he could see the slight swelling, the beginnings of fullness in her body. Her perfume rose to his nostrils, a hint of sweat mixed with a deep tang of a herb he did not recognise. He felt the shock of realisation; she is pregnant here beside me. What does Marie think?

He imagined his ex-wife's emphatic response, her dark curls shaking a furious negative, something he had often seen. She was ten years younger than him; perhaps her curls were greying by now. It was so long since he had seen her; how long? He could not think exactly.

'It's good to see you, Gabriella. How is… how are you, how is your health?'

'You mean, my pregnancy.' She was laughing at him. 'It is fine, especially now I have stopped being sick every day.'

'What about the father?'

'No, he was only the donor, the giver of the vital sperm. Don't look so upset, Walter. You are going to be a grandfather.'

Gabriella's father had vanished many years before. She had no contact with him and always professed not to care about him. Now she told Walter that Marie too wanted his own involvement.

'What shall we call you? Pop?'

'How has your mother taken it?'

'She's fine. Just glad I am getting on with it. She thought I was neglecting my body clock, you know, getting too old at thirty. So now she will get a chance to be a grandmother.'

Her happiness seemed extravagant to him but unstoppable. She was waiting for him to exclaim, to be glad, to care that a child was coming into the world who would be his, would belong to him. But be no blood relation. He was pleased for her. Also confused by the casual way she spoke of giving up work for a while, looking after the baby on her own. Celia had made the same declarations; it seemed these young women had no fear, no trepidation as they planned to step into parenthood. And no real understanding, he thought. Poor Celia. Gabby being already pregnant will be such a hard blow.

Gabby had another shock for him.

'I have got a partner, Walter. You haven't met her yet, but I hope you will. She is happy about the baby too. Yvette. She's lovely.'

'I didn't know. I thought you – the father – and you did have a boyfriend, wasn't his name Adam?'

'It is allowed these days, one or both, man or woman. It's not compulsory to choose just one gender.'

She was smiling gently at him, taking hold of his arm and giving it the lightest of squeezes.

'It happened, that's all. And I have had a few misses with men, including this one. More than one bad experience. So, falling for a woman, it feels right. And fun too.'

They sat in silence. Walter wanted to work out the timing of this event, the stranger, the new lover, when and how did it happen? He was sorry that he could not find the words to explain himself, how he was thinking. He smiled and hoped she would accept it as enough.

'Come on. I need to get home soon. So, you want to finish here, don't you. I'll leave you to plant some more. See you very soon.'

As she stretched herself up from the bench, she turned and said, 'How is that illegal getting on? Have you sent him off yet? Or found him someone else to help maybe?'

He had intended to go down to the Sanctuary Centre to see if there was anyone who could give advice to Amro. He had intended to tell him to go there himself. Somehow, though, the days and weeks had passed. Amro had started page turning his way through the collection of recipe books in the house. They began choosing a meal together, Walter writing a list of the ingredients and happy to try something new. Amro spent time in front of the bookshelves in the living room alcoves, scanning along the novels and the history books, the travel picture ones and the guides to a good healthy life which Linda had chosen, books once read and now left gathering dust in honour of their past lives.

One day Amro picked up a paperback and asked if he could borrow it to read.

Walter looked at what he had chosen. *The Woodlanders*.

'That's one of my favourite writers.'

'Hardy, it is a name I know,' Amro said. 'English literature. We love it in my country too.'

'That's a long, hard read, lad, for me, never mind you.'

'I can try. You like this? I will try it.'

'Try this one, if you want to. *Under The Greenwood Tree* – it's shorter, a bit less complicated. But I mean, the English is old fashioned. It's not easy. Try something else. It's a long time since I read these. Let me see what else we have for you to start with.'

'But I am better at reading than you think. I will try it.' He smiled at Walter to indicate he had not taken offence. Over the next few days, Walter watched with surprise. With a dictionary on one side, Amro read slowly, page by page with his finger hovering over lines, but with obvious relish, sometimes asking for help with a word or going back over a passage with Walter to assist with the meaning.

'I cannot understand all, my friend. No, you are right, it is hard, a bit strange. I like the way the words flow. And it reminds me of home. The fields, the work of the people,' he said after the first few afternoons of sitting by the window with the book open on his knee and the dictionary to hand. 'I wanted to go to the city, but I read this, and I think of my home in the village.'

'We shall have to go out for the day.' Walter was thrilled. 'When you can, of course. In the future.' For a moment he hesitated. What future was there ahead for Amro, for their friendship? He went on, 'I'll take you to the Dales, that's my countryside, where I like to walk. I love it there and it is a bit like Thomas Hardy.'

'That is marvellous. Is it like this story?'

'Well, I might be exaggerating, lad. No, it has changed a lot. But you will see fields, farms, rivers, hills – it is beautiful.'

'It is good to read,' Amro would say, putting the paper book marker Walter had given him in to hold his place. 'My English got worse before, now it is a bit better. I have been so long with my brain stopped. You know. It stops when you are… you can't think, you know, moving, moving, nothing to do, always on the, how you say, edges.'

Walter was quiet for a moment, acknowledging this.

'When you were living with your girlfriend here, did she read? Did she have books?'

'No, not she. She enjoyed life in the now. But, Walter, I was a teacher once. Not literature, of course. But I had students; I worked with ideas. The story is this man's ideas. Maths is ideas too, you know.'

Walter said to himself that he would start reading novels again. His brain had got lazy. Here was someone using another language so well. He must smarten up his own ideas.

In this way, the routine they had built between them continued peacefully, despite the fearful anticipation of the fortnightly trips into Leeds to the Home Office. Amro said little on those mornings, his face narrow and hard. When he came home, a breath of relief entered with him. He had not been stopped; he had not been taken into detention. The tension lifted. Then they acted for another period of time as if it would not happen again. Walter felt his own anxiety as a background to each of those days, but he put it aside as if it would die of its own accord.

Now Gabby was shaking her head at him. 'How long is it going to go on?'

'Tell you what. I'll ask around, see if I can get you advice – find out what it would be best to do. You can't just let it go on, doing nothing. Really, Walter, by avoiding the problem like this, you are going to get into trouble.'

He was grateful for her youthful strength, knowing her verdict was the right one. He nodded thanks before going back to put the last late spinach seeds in a careful, pre-watered row and updating his notebook before the day's end.

TWO

After the unnatural heat, the rains started. For three weeks, rain fell in continuous sheets, churning soil to mud, filling streams and brooks to run with force, creating ponds on every green verge. In some parts of the country, whole villages were marooned in lakes, when broiling rivers breached inadequate and neglected defences. Amro and Walter were pinned into the house. Walter broke a tenet of his retirement and put the television on in the daytime. The sound of rain was a backdrop to tea and sandwiches. On the plot, his vegetables responded with frantic growth and then collapse as the rain beat down beanpoles and flooded salad beds. Walter puddled in mud over his garden shoes to rescue what he could.

On a day the forecasters promised would be the first dry one, he and Frank set out for their summer walk in the Dales.

Gerry had said, 'No way, I'm not going out in that – it'll only rain again.' So it was the two of them, determined to keep to the annual routine and both feeling the urgent need of space and clean air. Walter had thought for one tiny moment that he might ask Amro along. Obviously, he couldn't do that; it would have to be another day, just with him.

It was dry under a grey sky, but the ground everywhere swelled like a hidden swamp under each footstep. The grass in all the fields was bright green in midsummer. The river had drowned itself. Trees spread reluctant arms into the fast brown water over the waving growth of sunken plants. It was hard to believe that the previous June they had watched the trickle left by drought in the same river. Their boots were soon clogged with thick clay.

They paused to lean on a gate and gazed over the wall at the view of the dale, green and grey, below them.

Frank said, 'It's strange to think that this landscape is man-made. Not natural at all.'

'I love it here.'

Walter and Linda had so often talked of coming to live in one of these villages, later on in life, to start every day with a view over the valley, the fields and lanes waiting for walks. He knew it was a dream which they would have lost as time rolled forwards. He still held the imagined cottage in his mind, could still see the corner where the road opened out to reveal the hills. He knew the living could be difficult here. He thought of the lean, hard-faced men, dark under their caps, whom he had watched at the Hawes Cattle Market once with Linda and Celia.

'But it wasn't always like this. Think of the miners slogging up there.' Above them, on the slope of the hill, the remains of the lead mining industry lay about in dark heaps and hollows. The prettiness of the farming landscape was a recent thing in history. Walter's family had been down into the stifling closeness of the coal mines, so he shrank from those ruins and what they made him imagine.

'Yeah. That was a tough time. The coffin road we're standing on must have been a busy one, eh. Carrying the dead along the valley to their grave, that was a hard walk,' Frank said.

'Who owns the land now anyway? There's not many of these farms are worked by them as owns them. Even though it's a national park it's all the big boys who own the fields. And they only come up here to shoot grouse.'

'And all the new money buys up the old barns – everywhere in the Dales it's flashy new conversions, isn't it.'

'They've got to have those big floor-to-ceiling windows so you can see the bed – or the bath! What's that about? No privacy at all. Don't they care that you, the plebs, might see them?' They laughed companionably.

'But rewilding, not this kind of farming, they say that's the future. For the climate. Getting rid of the sheep for a start. They have eaten all the green stuff that should be here. There would be trees without sheep. Apparently.'

'That's not going to happen.'

They stood in silent agreement, the dilemmas of their age half understood, greatly dreaded, the future only a dark question mark.

Walking on, they began a slow conversation about their families. Walter hesitated to say anything about Gabby, unsure of the words to use. In a gap left by his own reticence, he commented on the difficulty of keeping Ramadan when the days were so long, as it had started during the recent weather, when the heat had been so exhausting.

'Is this your bloke then? He's Muslim, is he?'

'He is not so strict, but he does do the fasting. He's had a couple of breaks when it was roasting out – had to have water.'

'I don't get this having strict rules for life business. Jews are the same, aren't they, no pork, meat and milk, all that. Catholics even. Wasn't your Marie a Catholic?

'Yes, but flexible. Lots of people don't keep the rules, are not orthodox or practising. Marie went to mass when she was bored or cross with me.'

Frank laughed.

'Muslims are just the same. There's some flexibility. Amro won't eat our meat – that's his real sticking point.'

Walter knew he had opened the topic and that Frank was waiting for more, to ask him questions, to be told by his friend what the situation was. He had intended to take Amro down to the Sanctuary Centre, for advice and help. But he could not explain or justify his wish that it should not change, that he wanted the days to go on as before, that the young man fitted into his life comfortably. There was danger in a change. He recognised his own selfish grasp in that thought.

'Janet has met him, she thinks.'

'Janet, how could she? What do you mean?' He remembered as he spoke that Amro had said he had been down once to the Centre.

'I told her what I know about him, what you said about him being Egyptian, not Palestinian.'

Walter stopped on the path.

'How do you know that?'

'Because you told me, mate. One night over a bevy.' A few

beers too many, was this what had happened, and he had no memory of it?

'So, I described him? I couldn't have told you what he looks like; I'm sure I didn't. Did I?'

'I've seen him, going up your street, had to be him, foreign-looking and young and so on.'

So others could know about his visitor, other passers-by, the neighbours, anyone.

'She thinks he came for advice and saw their legal person, gives immigration advice once a week. People queue up for ages to see him as he is good apparently.'

'What advice did he get?'

'Oh, she doesn't know that; that's confidential unless they want to say. And she didn't know him well. Just gave him some food for a few weeks. They get a tenner too if they are on the list, refused and can't work, hardly enough to live on, but it helps.'

So that was part of the missing times, when Amro had lived who knows how. He had been helped then, at least a little.

The two men walked on, the field ahead stony and uneven, with a path indistinct and the direction only recognisable by the small yellow sign on a stile in a far corner.

Later they resumed talking of their families and Walter confided the story about Gabriella. He admitted his confusion and doubt about the child without a father and his stepdaughter living with a woman.

'It's all different from our day,' Frank said. Walter had said nothing about Celia and IVF. He knew he was a coward.

'Your two are alright though.'

'Thought so, but Olivia is having a tough time now, talks about leaving him, the wedding only a few years past. All that money and fuss, it cost us a fortune, Janet worked on all the details for months, everything had to be just so, all co-ordinated colours, the whole business, you wouldn't credit it. Now, she says he is boring and nasty with it. Janet's very upset about the children; our Rosie is still a baby. I don't know. I think she might end up living back with us.'

'What do you feel about that?'

'What do you think? There's no way Janet is going to tell her she can't come, and my opinion doesn't count.'

'What about the boy, your Samuel?'

'Still single, lots of friends, partying, never shows any sign of settling down and there's no girlfriend that lasts for very long. Not going to be any grandkids there.'

Frank has always spoken fondly and without criticism of his children. He and Janet are conventional and quiet, their two children successful and settled – this has been Walter's understanding up until now.

When they were back in the car park, cleaning the sticky mud from their boots, taking off layers of clothing and slinging backpacks into the boot, Frank said to Walter, 'You must bring him down to the Centre soon. Or there could be trouble. You know the immigration police take people away.'

'No, he's going to the Home Office in Leeds now. If he goes into detention, it will be from there. Every fortnight he has to go and report.'

'Has he got a solicitor?'

'He's had one. I'll have to ask him about it.'

His old friend settled into the driver's seat, turned on

the engine and, as the car began to move forwards, he said, 'Walter, you must do something. Can't let it ride like this. The police might turn up at your house any day, even if he is going in to report. It's hard, but he can't stay at yours forever, can he?'

THREE

He stirred the soaked porcini mushrooms into the rice and added a ladleful more of the stock which was bubbling away. Parsley was chopped and parmesan grated ready; he had a large lump of butter to add. Gabriella loved risotto so he was glad to stand, patiently moving the grains of rice round and round, watching them soak up the oil-scented stock and the mushroom liquor. She was quiet, drinking water from a large wine glass as, 'It helps with the illusion and compensates for the loss,' she said brightly. He had asked her to supper to speak to Amro, to bring the fruits of her research to help him. But Amro was out. Ramadan was in its last days. He spent much of each day resting and talking to friends on the phone, before leaving every evening for the mosque. Today, instead of warming up a plate that Walter had left for him, Amro had gone to break his fast with a communal meal, called an iftar, at the mosque. Walter had forgotten to ask him to eat here to meet Gabby. He would not be home until late, as he could not eat until night fell and the mosques announced permission.

'It's okay, I can tell you what I was told by the expert my friend knows. It's nice to see you anyway.' She looked even more round, her belly in a thin dress meeting the edge of the tabletop. 'I wanted to ask you, have you told Celia about me, about the baby?'

'Yes, just yesterday.'

'How did she take it?'

Walter thought of how she had said nothing in response, the waiting for her to speak again, his sorrow for her. He must ring her again, go over to see her. He took hold of his own glass and drank, glad of the pause and the rush of the cold wine.

'It's hard for her, you know. She's tried IVF and is waiting for another go.'

'I knew about the IVF, Walter. It was a secret, but she did tell me afterwards. So that's why I haven't seen her and haven't said about the baby.'

'But now look at me. I'm enormous for six months, huge. So, she has to know.'

The risotto was eaten, the dishes cleared, and they were sitting over raspberry ice cream, made with fruit from his own bushes, when Gabby talked to him about Amro.

'You must tell him, Walter. You are burying your head in the sand. So is he. Any minute now he will be taken into detention, again you say, then he will be deported forcibly. It is better to take this decision so he has a chance then to make a life for himself.'

'He can't go back. He left because it was so dangerous for him. His family told him to go. He is frightened to go back there.' Walter continued. 'He had such a terrible time getting here. You haven't heard all that, have you? We can't imagine that journey ourselves. We couldn't do it. He can't go back as if nothing has happened.'

'The Home Office says it is now safe. The reaction to the uprising, the Arab Spring, it is over. The country is quiet; there is stable government.'

'The Home Office, what do they know?' This sounded ridiculous to his own ears. Gabby's pregnancy had softened her voice and brought her a new gentleness. She was sympathetic but insistent. He wanted her to leave, to process this news by himself. She leaned over the table and took his hand.

'You must take him down to the Sanctuary Centre, let someone there tell him the truth. He is an educated man; he is wasting his life here, Walter. You must see that.'

There were shadows on the lawn now. The long evenings were closing slowly in on themselves, the dusk drawing nearer each day. In his notebook, he had a list of tasks to do on his patch; there were still beans, the runners in full burst, though the French ones were growing tough and stringy now; he had the strawberry bed to clear for new plants. He could work in the evening for another couple of weeks if he chose. But his body was reluctant. He sank onto a chair once she had left, leaned back and shut his eyes.

FOUR

'He is a liar, Dad,' her voice shrilled. 'You are protecting him when you know he lied, to the authorities, to you. He has been working on the black market – he is not allowed to work! He has been here for years when he has no right to be.'

'Why doesn't he have the right? He is an educated person. He wants to contribute. He wants to work, to have his own life. It is not his fault that he is in this position.' He knew as he said it that she would come back sharply.

'Not his fault! He did not have to lie. He decided to say he is something he is not. He only confessed because he had to. The Home Office know about him now and you should face up to it.'

'He told Gabby about his situation, who he is. He told her because he was tired and lonely. He didn't have to say anything to her.'

'Dad, this is impossible. Gabby agrees with me for what it is worth.'

'The two of you are ganging up, are you?'

'You are feeding him, giving him money, I bet. Where does he go when he leaves the house? Do you even know?'

Walter wanted to close the call. He hated the tone she used to berate him. It was unfair, not her business, she sounded so angry, so judgemental of her parent. Why couldn't she see that he knows what he is doing, why couldn't she trust her father to know what's best?'

'He is taking you for a ride, Dad. You must see that.'

'Celia, you do not have to be so judging. Think about him a little. I am sorry you get so cross about me being kind to someone.'

This was the strongest he could be in response. It was so hard to be straight with one's children. She was quiet for a breath.

'Dad, I actually rang you about something else. Something important.'

He wanted to say, 'This is important to me. And you raised the topic first.'

'How are you?' he said.

'I am just fine. I do have some news.' Her voice had softened. Warmth flowed towards him for the first time. 'Can you guess my news?'

He said nothing, unsure of the game, if it was a game.

'I have started the IVF again.' She made each syllable sound separately. *Again*, he thought. *She is risking all that pain again. Another disaster. I must be pleased; I must be optimistic.*

'That's wonderful, love.'

'Yes, it is. I have another chance, Dad. I've met a man too, Art, he is so great.'

Walter's spirits rose to his face. He smiled down the phone. She had a boyfriend, someone to be a father.

'He will help, him and his partner Rich. A gay couple, Dad. They will be my baby's family too. So, you don't have to worry so much about me being a single parent.'

Walter felt he could not digest this additional information. He felt confusion swamp him again.

'Why don't you come over for a meal. Come and see me, I'd love to see you.' He put enthusiasm and persuasion into his voice. If he could get her to see Amro, to talk to him, perhaps she would relent and help her father and his friend.

'Why? You want me to see your refugee, is that it?' Her voice was harsh again.

'Celia, there is no need for you to speak to me like that.' He was angry, but she was right. He felt shame. How far apart they seemed. 'We don't see much of each other. We never get a chance to talk, do we? Yes, I would like you to meet Amro properly. But you are my daughter, and you have lots happening.' This sounded so lame. 'I want to see you.'

'Then come over here, Dad. I am working from home on Friday and will finish early. So, if you come, we'll eat out or in, your choice, and we can talk.'

Walter's moment to be brave had arrived. This is what he told himself as the road flattened over the moor two days later. On the back seat there was a casserole dish and three smaller containers. "I'll bring dinner" he told Celia by text. He carried them up her stairs in a large bag, going carefully step by step with his precious cargo. She looked surprised as he unloaded the bag and set out his wares on the kitchen surface.

'This is Egyptian food, cooked for us by Amro, my friend and, at the moment, my housemate.'

He saw that Celia was curling her lip.

'He wants you to taste his country. You know he is a good cook. And he went to get us meat, halal meat in fact, especially for this dish.'

'Halal meat?' She looked alarmed. 'What is it then?'

'It is lamb cooked in spices with rice and tomato sauce. It is called fatta or something like that and it is something he would eat at home in his village.'

'Lamb?' She made it sound as if the meat was a threat.

'You still eat some meat, don't you? I thought you did.' He felt a tremor of uncertainty. Perhaps he had got it really wrong.

'Yes, I do. Less but… okay, Dad.' She opened the main pot and peered in, sniffing as the spiced air rose.

'And he is still fasting you know, a couple more days till it ends with Eid,' he was proud of his new knowledge, 'so he made this although he couldn't eat it himself. While he was fasting today. He made it for us.'

She said nothing, putting the mixtures into different pans without comment.

'Are you feeling alright?' He looked at her slim frame with surprise each time he thought of her being pregnant. She did not look strong enough to carry a child.

'Yeah, I'm fine.' Brisk and excluding from further questions.

'Shall we heat it up and have a drink first?' He needed a large drink for courage even though he was driving. *I must not fail now*; he almost said it aloud. 'He has made a dip too, for us to nibble on, with pitta breads even.'

Now he sounded too keen, desperate. He must not

spend the evening talking about Amro. The food was a gift Amro had wanted to make, suggested with enthusiasm and pleasure in his ability to do so. Amro had offered it as he believed it would itself bring peace. Walter knew to dissolve the barrier of cold air between him and his only daughter would take more than spices tasting rich on the tongue. He had resolved to be different today, to break his habit of restraint, of respectful, but self-serving, distance.

Celia stayed cool. She brought him beer, a bottle he didn't like but accepted. She laid out the pittas in a basket and spooned the dip into a pretty bowl. She poured herself a tonic water with ice.

There was a silence in the room, a heavy quiet broken only by the sound of his beer glass as he set it down and the light crash of her ice as she shook her drink. It came to him that he must overcome the struggle with words and let her know how he felt. At least some of what he felt.

'Celia, you know, I miss your mother so much.'

She glanced up from her glass. Her eyes were wide.

'Sometimes I see her. Yes, I do see her, just waiting in the distance, not so far but not near enough. She looks as beautiful as she was.'

'You miss Mum. You didn't miss her. You moved on. Sharpish.' Her accusation stung. He swallowed. How could he go on? 'Do you see her? Mum, really?'

'I miss her so much. I missed her when I was married to Marie.' She sniffed disbelievingly. 'Yes really. I was lonely, Celia, can't you understand that?'

'So now you've got a new son too. What's his name? Is it his real name? Has he got more than two?'

'Celia, please.' The purpose of his visit, the reason he was here, was slipping away.

'You can't blame me, Dad. You didn't tell me about this man. And he is living in our house, your house. What really do you know about him?'

'I know he taught maths in a university, that he likes English literature, yes he can read it, quite slowly of course, he is someone you would like, you would like him if you met him properly. And he is not a son for me. He is a friend, someone I can help. Am trying to help.'

She dropped her gaze and said nothing in reply.

'Anyway, please let's talk about, about your mum, not Amro, that's not why I'm here.' There was a pause in the room. 'I did marry Marie quite quickly.' She made a snorting sound which he ignored. 'I was lonely, and I was weak too. I admit that. Marie liked me; it was easy. Easier to be in a couple again. You weren't there; you needed to be away. Of course, you did.'

'My work was here. Is here.'

'Yes, I am not saying you had any responsibility, that you should have been with me. But I missed you too.'

'Dad, why are you starting to talk like this?' She got to her feet and started towards the kitchen.

'I am just trying to tell you the truth. We have never talked about all this, have we? We have to try. Please, love, sit down.'

She folded herself into the chair opposite him, her blonde head lowered and her feet in trainer socks restlessly moving back and forwards as if she could not still them. He thought how thin she was and how young.

'Think how your mother would be so pleased for you that you are going to have, hope to have, a child. She would have been so delighted, she would want to be here with you and support you. Now you've only got a fairly useless old man.' He tried, but failed, to make this sound light-hearted.

'I wish she was here.' It sounded so bleak that he felt tears rise in his own eyes.

'Yes, we both do, lovely girl. But she left you a model of being a mother, didn't she? You will be as good a mother as she was. You can be proud of who you are. I am proud of you.' He had never said this to her before.

'But you married Marie so quickly, how can you say you miss her?'

'I was lonely, lost; I was offered companionship. Is that so bad?'

'And a new family.' She was crying, soft tears on both cheeks.

'Lovely daughter, you are my family. No one replaces you. No one replaced your mother.'

He moved from his chair and crouched awkwardly by her feet. He held out his arms. She was stiff at first, her arms crossed and her chest held away from him, resisting the embrace. Slowly, he felt her body soften and he gave her his chest; his arms held her tighter. As his tears mingled with hers, father and daughter leant into each other and at last were comforted.

FIVE

The young men in the doorway stepped back for him, smiling and nodding politely. He pushed through hesitantly. There was a reception table to one side where two women, one with grey hair whom he thought he might know and another younger person in bright clothing, were writing names down on pieces of paper and handing out slips. The grey hair looked up as he approached.

'Please wait,' she said briskly. 'You are after these,' indicating the crowds in the narrow hallway.

Confused, he stood aside. It was mostly men around him, from all the countries of the world, he thought. One loud individual, speaking perfect English, was saying to the desk that he was Russian. There were two women in headscarves sitting against the wall; one was holding a baby close to her chest; the other had her eyes closed. A toddler, trying out speed with the excitement of new legs, burst out of another room. A tall African scooped him gently up, laughed at his squeals of protest and took him back. Walter realised that there were two rooms full of activity and people. He was taking up valuable time and space. As he turned to leave, Janet appeared on the stairs.

'Walter. It is you. How are you? Are you here about your lodger? Don't worry, we have his records. Come up with me.' When he indicated the women at the table, she shrugged and said, 'You are a visitor. You can sign in later.' He was conscious that all the people were watching him go up with her, a privilege they were waiting for.

There was one large room upstairs which he realised was the meeting room for the Quakers. The Sanctuary was using this place for its work. In the centre there was a circle of chairs with Bibles on a low table. But now the room had other purposes. In each corner, there was a folding table that had become a desk where urgent conversations in low voices were being conducted.

'Sit here in the middle; we will be out of everyone's way, Walter. You can see, we have volunteers here sorting out all sorts of problems – money, work, travel, family reunion – you name it, we get it.'

'Where are they all from?'

'Everywhere. Lots of Iranians at the moment, Kurdish Iraqis, Eritreans of course, but everywhere really.' She had not mentioned Egyptians.

'And legal advice, can they get that here?' This was what he was interested to know.

'We have one advisor who works on the major cases and two others who have initial training.'

'An advisor, not a solicitor, a real lawyer.'

'No, they are volunteers, as everyone is. But our main

advisor, Stanley, he is outside on the landing, did you see him as we came up the stairs? He works under the guidance and supervision of a lawyer, a proper lawyer, and refers cases to her if necessary. So, if your young man comes here, he will have to wait like everyone else, but we will make sure he is seen and gets advice. Stanley is very good.'

'Doesn't it cost to see the proper lawyer?'

'If they need to see her, and only if, it's pro bono – she does it for free.'

He was unsure of what to say. This Janet was so bright, so organised. There was no sign of the woman who compulsively fiddled with her hair, which today, in any case, was tied back severely in a ponytail.

'Let me show you round.'

He followed downstairs, where the group of people waiting seemed to be the same, into the other spaces. 'See, we have English tables, craft over there, free tea and coffee, and we get buns and things from the shops; here is the Health Visitor.' The rooms were crowded, noisy with talk; no one looked at him; they were all busy. Janet walked him through clusters of people, waving at some and stopping to shake hands with others. He was an awkward extra in this place where everyone had an intention, a need, a task. He was embarrassed and also impressed.

'So, bring him down; we will look after him. He knows us anyway. He came here last year for the food bank. We wondered what had happened to him.'

'The food bank?'

'That happens out of the cupboard a bit later. We put the destitute on a list and I do that. Oh,' looking at her watch, 'I'll have to start soon, yes, I won't be long.' This last to an anxious man who plucked at her sleeve in passing.

As he walked back through the town, Walter thought that a pro bono lawyer was not going to be as good as one you paid. Illogical to think that but still, he did. Perhaps he could raid his savings and pay for someone to give Amro the best advice he could get.

His phone was vibrating in his pocket. It was Celia.

'Dad, are you free on Saturday? I'd like you to come over and have lunch with me and meet Art. Please say yes.'

SIX

The noodle bar was busy with Saturday shoppers, pairs and groups, bags bumping into your shoulder as they passed your table. It was hard to hear what Celia and her companion were saying.

He strained forwards to be introduced to the friend who said, 'Hi, I'm Art and I am so pleased to meet you, Walter.' His handshake was firm, confident.

The man was wearing a dark blue shirt which made you aware of how blue his eyes were; he was tall, had short, smart hair, not the shaved head so many sported; he was clean shaven, presentable certainly. Walter had clung for so long to the hope that she would find a new man, a person to make a settled life with and the magic person she might have children with. He had put this hope aside, but it was still there. Now he had to understand that this man here was the new sperm donor, a man who was not only donating sperm, giving life, but wanting to have the child they now knew was on the way, wanting to be the co-parent, whatever that might mean.

'Dad, what would you like? There's lots of choice.' Celia seemed relaxed but also excited. Her hair was scraped up into one of the buns so fashionable now. He liked her hair softer, falling around her face.

He glanced again at the plastic board which served as a menu. It was in hideously bright colours, so it was hard to distinguish the difference in the dishes. The words jumped around. The noise of voices rising up to the ceiling, with some kind of music he could not distinguish overlaying the racket, was making him uncomfortable.

He smiled and said, 'You choose for me. You know I love this kind of food. Whatever you think.'

Celia turned to Art. 'Dad is a great cook. He can do a mean stir fry himself.' She looked well, her skin clear and her eyes bright.

It was a silly name, but he had a pleasant, courteous manner. He smiled frequently at Celia; he offered to buy Walter a beer. He refused, 'I'm driving,' but later regretted it. The noodles were horribly sweet, and the tang of Asian lager would have helped. He wanted to ask Celia's advice about Amro and finding a lawyer for him, but this was not the moment or the place. He tried to calm himself and enjoy the occasion, whatever it was. He felt inadequate and bemused. His daughter was happy. That would have to do for today.

On the drive home, he reasoned with himself, unsuccessfully. He supposed he had managed to present an accepting front in the noodle bar. He had said how much he had enjoyed the noodles. He nodded his way through the explanations, kept a steady gaze. He had wished them good luck. He kissed his daughter and swiftly hugged her as he was leaving. He had not shaken the man's hand again. That seemed too much.

So now he had a stepdaughter with a baby on the way, conceived in passing by someone whose name he was not to know, and perhaps the baby would not know, and a daughter who was having another IVF procedure, expensive, difficult and uncertain after last time, with a man she had recently met online, who was a gay man living with another man. This gay man with the too short name, Art. Co-parent, where does this word come from, is that not what all parents do?

He had the full set, potential grandchildren brought up by gay partners, one female, one male. Two daughters with children (possibly in Celia's case) and not a heterosexual man, not a father, in sight.

SEVEN

'Please come with me, Walter sir. It is a great celebration. Lots of people will be there, from the churches too, the community will join us. It is nearly time for the Eid. Everyone will be excited. I would be happy to have you there.'

Amro was thin; he had taken the fasting very seriously near the end. The days had been quiet, and Amro had spent much more time than usual out of the house, at the mosque or with friends in the town. Now the month was almost over and there would be a feast in the old community centre.

'We start with a little water and a date. You must not eat at first, however much you want to. Then there will be so much food. Delicious food. One of the restaurants in town is donating it. You will love it, sir.'

'Thank you. I will come.' It would be churlish not to show his gratitude, to be pleased to be included. 'Do I have to wait until nearly ten o'clock then to eat? I'll do my best. First, can we have a chat, my friend.'

He wanted to see how much he did know about this

person, his experience and his situation. He wanted to ask him to say again how he had arrived, why he had lied so unnecessarily, what did he think was going to happen now at the Home Office interviews? He had so many questions he had not asked before.

Amro was cheerful, chatty, made Walter tea in a pot, the way he had learnt, raising his hands with a smile to say it was alright to drink it in front of him. It was not long now until the moment of feasting.

'Why do you think fasting is good? Why do you do it? Because the Koran says so?'

'Because it is good practice. It is hard, but your mind can focus when you deny the body. It is good to think inside yourself, to reflect on yourself. It makes you think too about all those who cannot eat and drink easily or enough. The discipline joins you to others in the world.'

This answer left Walter sitting over his tea, gazing at his guest.

When he asked him again about his journey, the mood in the room altered. Amro's charming face stiffened. With great hesitation and reserve, he told him that he had travelled on his own when he received the message that the police would come for him as they already had for many friends and colleagues at the university. He had reached the French coast, where he spent "seven months, eight days" in the Calais camp. Every night he tried to get on a lorry. Every night with many others, he was chased away. 'If the French police caught you, they beat you, with sticks and fists. I was beat so many times by those policemen.'

At last one night, he managed to climb into a lorry. He

hid under boxes of medical supplies with another man, a stranger to him. They had no food or water for the hours they were confined in a stifling dark place, listening to changes in the engine, hearing the scream of the brakes when it stopped and being jostled helplessly by the boxes shifting with the movement. Not knowing where they were or when they had arrived, the light and noise flooding in was a shock that made his whole body shake. The officers pulled them both roughly onto the tarmac. 'I could not see properly; I could not think. I had not eaten for so long, nothing to drink for so long. I did not take anything with me, just my clothes and my papers. They took me into an office, the lights so bright; they asked me questions. I could not say anything. I had my papers hidden. I was frightened, so frightened, Walter. I had to hide myself. Then I said I was from Palestine because that is the worst place.'

When he had finished this account, Amro sat with clenched hands and bowed head.

Walter blew out a long breath. 'Sorry, I don't know what to say.'

'It is fine. You are a good person.'

'Tell me the rest, Amro. Since you have been here. You have been refused, twice you told me – the whole Palestinian thing. You did have a British girlfriend?'

'She is Polish. She liked me at first and I was exciting for her perhaps.' Briefly, his face recovered its confidence, the handsome man remembering.

'I lived in her flat for many months. We had a good time. Though I did not like her drinking. She worked; she is a bus driver.'

Walter thought perhaps in the past or even recently, he had been on a bus driven by this person, Amro's girlfriend.

'One day she will go back to Poland with some money. Now with what has happened, with Europe, maybe she has to go back soon. I don't know. She doesn't answer my calls.'

'You have been in detention once. When was that?'

'When my girlfriend was fed up with me, I had to live on people's floors. Moving around. You have to. Someone told the police. They came for me.'

Amro rose up, walked around the room, rubbing his hands, his head lowered. He stood by the window.

'It was not for long then, only two months. I don't know why. They let me out. I think, that's it. But when they came for me the second time, I could not go. I told you about that. I could not go back into a cell. I will never forget what it was like. So, I ran.'

You are still running, Walter thought. All through the months his own life had been peacefully proceeding, he had been safe and comfortable, while the young man had been trying to find a place to be secure, to put his feet down firmly on a path which kept giving way in front of him.

'When we met, you know, Walter, sir, you found me in your garden, my refuge. I was running away from detention.'

'But the police did detain you after the car wash. They let you out, quite quickly?'

'I did not go to a centre. I don't know why; it was not for long. No reason is given. But they have me now – I have to report to the Home Office. You know.'

'They may detain you again. One of these days when you go into Leeds. They may just take you.'

'Yes. I pray they will not.'

It was a long time since Walter had prayed. The last had been a prayer of anger and supplication to all the gods of the sky as he held Linda's hand through that last terrible night. He could not now put his faith in the power of prayer.

EIGHT

When he was a young man, Walter had imagined a steady, unbroken progression from student in a drab bedsit to senior civil servant and family man with several children around him, dependent on his support. He had thrown off the obligatory short phase of long hair and pot smoking to embrace responsibility and serious labour over maps and files, conformity and attendance to the system. His parents had instilled in him the necessity to break out of the working-class limitations they had had and to soar higher. He achieved part of the dream. He had a pension from a solid history of local government positions. He had learned to do without many other things. He had discovered he did not need a crowd of children; his one daughter delighted him enough. Linda's quiet grace in the world had given him the perspective to accept his final lack of promotion, so far and no further. He had built himself a sense of satisfaction in exactly where he was, his feet on the ground in front of him. Linda's death had left him utterly bereft, adrift, until Marie swallowed him up into her warm and insistent arms, cajoling and smothering, offering him an energetic bed and release from himself.

Now one early morning of late summer Walter lay with an unaccustomed reluctance to start his day. The quiet routine life he had constructed over ten years, since the brief period of life with Marie, seemed to have no purpose. He could not focus on the planned arrival of the two babies. It seemed these events had nothing to do with him, were outside his influence, even his knowledge. Both women were expecting his involvement, his excitement; both rang him with updates on the pregnancy. Gabby's baby was a boy. She was nearing the last two months, so she was full of anticipation and also complaints about how uncomfortable she was. He worried about Celia in a detached, bemused fashion. Her calls were all about the contract she and Art had worked out, the way they would share responsibility and time with the child, now known to be a girl. He found it hard to listen to this practical, detailed approach to being a parent, so cold. Her assertions that she would need him to be an active grandparent seemed meaningless to him. Did she even believe it herself? Perhaps it was that he could not imagine how he would have the energy or be able to sustain the interest. A grandchild was a cause for joy. A new life, a new beginning – cliches, he thought. Not a new life for me. Lying in bed, he said to himself that he had not signed a contract. He was a free man, an old man who had already fulfilled his duties in the world. So many memories, some found and some lost, stretched out in flashes, bright one minute, blurred the next. He could only see part of what had been. He felt the years behind him as a burden, a weight pushing him forwards, a weight he could not shift nor embrace.

Energetic and lovely, Sue's image came to him again this morning. She continued to be friendly, stopping to talk on the plot, asking his advice. He was a little ashamed now of the way he had enjoyed imaginings of her before. This delightful person was his friend, trusting, interested, warm. More than once, he had nearly stepped one foot further and asked her out for a drink. But he hovered on the words and knew enough to stop. He had no right to ask for more. And he did not want to be an old fool.

One duty preoccupied his thinking. Celia had called it "voluntary repatriation". 'That is the best for him,' she had said. The idea of telling Amro that he must go back to the place he had escaped from, with such difficulty, such fear and suffering, seemed impossible. The story Amro had told returned to him as images he could not lose. He had a sense that there was a dark line ahead, beyond which he could not see. But the precarious edge which Amro lived on, the threat of this life in Walter's house suddenly stopping, with a swift descent into a detention cell, that threat was real. The peace could evaporate any day. Walter must face the trouble. He must talk to him, give the advice, tell him to go to the Centre; he knew it was unavoidable now.

Going to the communal meal, which he had learnt to call an iftar, had cheered Walter. Beforehand he had felt uncertain, as if he would be a misfit, an oddity, someone who did not belong. The community centre hall was filled with long trestle tables and plastic chairs, with a buffet of hot food along one wall. As he walked in, he recognised, with a small sense of surprise, many faces he knew, from the Pakistani community, from the pub crowd, some of his neighbours. Frank and Janet steered through to meet him. The hall was filled with colour. Many of the women were dressed in elaborate embroidered clothes, and many men who wore denim or work suits every day had changed into the white shalwar kameez. Walter was glad he had chosen to wear his own best white shirt. Children ran among the legs giggling or leaned wearily against adults. Amro clearly knew many of the people there. He looked relaxed, moving around the groups of men, shaking hands, greeting and being greeted.

There was a waiting period, with calm expectancy among the worshippers, until the mullahs gave the say so, how Walter could not see. Some of the younger men went off to pray, but everyone else sat down, reached for the water and began to share the large dates set out in bowls along the length of each table. There was no rush, no haste. Trays of spicy food were offered first to others; it was a feast of gentle enjoyment and generosity. Amro came to sit with Walter, sliding into a chair next to him at the last moment. Janet nodded to him, and he gave her his charming smile. Frank looked across and said, 'Hello, good to meet you.'

Days had passed now since Eid when Amro had been out of the house for two days, going from house to house, he told Walter, from party to party. 'Whose house?' Walter enquired.

'Lots of different people,' was the answer. 'Iranians, Kurdish, even Pakistani, I know them all.'

Walter saw another man flourishing out of the refugee sleeping on an allotment, a confident, sociable man. Someone who could easily make friends, who moved freely among people who enjoyed his company and who saw him as a person with something to offer. He thought this was how Amro had been as a teacher, moving among his students with the power to influence and impress. He could have been that person in this city.

Today Walter intended to speak to his guest. He committed himself to the difficulty and the pain of the task. The best thing to do for his friend turned out to be also the worst thing. They had come to the edge of the cliff. The peace of these days was a precarious illusion. He had kept a secret flame of hope. In his life, the aim had always been to keep quiet, to avoid trouble. Walter thought himself someone not suited to action. That day with the apples, he had started to act and as the friendship grew, as he understood what this man faced, he had stepped forwards. Followed his instincts. Somewhere the belief that Amro could stay, have a life, join life, had been growing unbidden with a sense that he, Walter, could help. Now this was failure. Failure for Amro and failure of his own adventure. It must be faced.

He planned to shop for a special meal; he would buy halal meat for the first time himself and research a recipe from Egypt. He would talk to Amro over that supper. He would tell him what Celia and Gabby both advised, from their understanding, from experts in immigration law, what they had suggested to him was the right way, the only way, in the asylum seeker's best interests. He would not say anything about the hostility still in Celia's approach or the warning Gabby had given that he was liable to be detained at any moment. He would accompany him down to the Sanctuary Centre in the Quaker Meeting House and support him when he was told by their legal advisor it was time to go. Gabby had rejected his idea about paying for a "proper" solicitor, as she said the advice would be the same, whether free or very expensive. He had not mentioned this to Celia as she was certain to defend her profession and think its practitioners worth any expense.

So, on this cloudy late August day when the first flares of colour were showing high up on the horse chestnut trees in the city streets, he prepared himself to do this thing. Over a cup of tea and a boiled egg, he waited for Amro to be up and about. The morning was ticking by before he heard him moving.

'Good morning,' in as bright a tone as he could find. 'Is everything alright?' Amro looked as if he was unwell, his skin a different shade, his eyes heavy and downcast.

'I have something to tell you, Walter.'

'I have something to talk to you about, lad. Let me get you some coffee and we can say, whatever it is.'

'First, please let me say. I talked to your friend yesterday evening.'

'My friend? Which one?' He kept his tone light, but he felt an ominous darkening.

'The lady. Janet. She told me that I must go and get advice from the Centre again because she knows my situation.' They sat opposite each other in silence.

'Amro, I am sorry, I told her husband, Frank; he is my friend. I didn't mean for it to go further.' He could not finish because he, of course, might have thought that Frank would tell his wife and that his wife volunteered in the Centre, knew Amro by name, so, of course, she would have an opinion. He had held his secret to keep it safe. To keep this friend safe. And to keep this friend with him.

'In a way, it is relief. When I told your daughter Gabriella, I saw a load go from my mind. I am an Egyptian. I am a man from my country. I have the papers. I am a lecturer in maths and geography. I have degrees, references. I have an Egyptian passport.' He stiffened in his chair, lifted his head and gave Walter a smile which said so many things.

'I can work. I want to work. I am not a criminal.'

'They say you must go back. That is the advice they will give you there.'

'I cannot go back. It is impossible.'

'The Home Office says it is safe now. They have an agreement that you will be safe. If you go, if you choose to go, they will give you the fare and money, quite bit of money, to start you off.'

'I want a life here. I have wasted these years, years and years. I have done no harm. Let me work, let me have a place, let me stay.'

The two friends sat in the kitchen as the light lengthened. Amro's plea hung useless, unheard, the plea of thousands who flee and end on a far shore, unwanted and turned away.

NINE

It was a slow morning at the Centre. Walter and Amro were there early, but the queue to see the legal advisors was already long. Amro put his name down on the grey-haired woman's list, took a slip with his number and they both stood in the hallway to wait. After a little while, Amro went outside for air. It was cool with a breeze that caught you around the neck, so it was only the smokers who waited in the paved garden off the street. Walter wondered if he was going to smoke. He would have liked to join him, felt he could manage a cigarette himself. But he must stay rooted, to save the place in the queue, to make sure Amro was not missed, not overlooked. The space was stuffy, warming up from so many bodies, all of them fearful, tense. He was the outsider here, the one who did not need a refuge.

Janet came through the bodies with a man who was holding a sheaf of papers. She saw him and waved, 'Will be back in a minute,' then went up the stairs. She had the same urgent energy as everyone else. Walter felt he was stiff, expectant, uneasy despite his privilege. Janet was down again in a minute, walked past him again, her face preoccupied until a woman spoke to her and she stopped. She went into the cafe room with the woman, briefly throwing Walter a smile over her shoulder. 'Good to see you here,' she said.

When Amro's number was called at last, an hour of waiting later, they both climbed the stairs to the first landing behind one of the brightly dressed volunteers. She indicated the table on the right where the legal advisor sat with a laptop and several cardboard files. He was a man of indeterminate age, maybe Walter thought in his fifties, with a crumpled shirt. He had a long, kind face and wore hearing aids. He stood up to shake hands.

'Hello, I'm Stanley. How can I help?' Walter started to introduce himself, but he shook his head. 'You're the host? Okay, let me talk to Amro.' He held out his hand for Amro's papers. He knew who the applicant was and had no interest in Walter's status. *Host*, Walter thought to himself. *Am I a host?* It was a pleasing word but left so much out.

'So tell me the story, Amro Elmary,' Stanley asked, and Amro began. He said nothing about his journey or the French police, just that he had said the wrong thing when they pulled him out of the lorry for interrogation. He had made a mistake because he thought authorities in the UK would be sympathetic to anyone from Palestine.

Stanley shook his head with his eyebrows raised.

'So, let's get this straight. You have been here nearly six years, is that right? And you have been through a solicitor? You have been trying to prove you are Palestinian?'

Amro nodded.

'And a solicitor has been trying on your behalf? You have been to London to see the Palestinian authorities, with a solicitor?'

Amro nodded. Walter squirmed in his chair. He wanted to interrupt, to say something to defend his friend. Stanley ignored him completely.

'So, you have been lying to everyone – for years?'

Amro said nothing. Again, he nodded his head.

'A hard life, living a falsehood.' This was a flat statement, in the same level tone he had used throughout. 'It's a pity.' Now he glanced at Walter. 'A shame because if you had told them the truth, that you are from Egypt, you had a chance of asylum.'

In the shocked silence that followed, he sat back from his table, thoughtfully fiddling with one of his ears. Walter saw the tiny aid was dislodged slightly until Stanley pushed it back.

'How could that be?' he found his voice to ask.

'Are you hosting this young man? Yes? Well, he came in, Amro, you came in,' turning again to him, 'you came in just after the Arab Spring clampdown. The Home Office recognised the political situation there had become very dangerous and anyone who had protested was at risk. So, you would have had an easy ride, a fairly easy ride I should say.'

Amro got to his feet. His face was pale, and his hands trembled as he held one out to Stanley.

'Thank you. I must go.' He stumbled on the words before walking away, down the stairs, pushing past people who were coming up, and went out of the front door into the street.

'He's left his papers behind. I take it you can give them back to him.'

'It's hard to accept. He made a mistake, a stupid mistake.' Walter stared at the advisor, willing him to say something different. 'After all he has been through. You know, he is an educated person.'

'Yes, I can see that. But I'm afraid he has burnt his boats. He would have had a chance if he had told the truth then. I have to say, only a chance. It is never easy for asylum seekers. But he has lied and that is that.'

'What if he explained now, told them the truth? He has his papers there, you can see, he even has an Egyptian passport.'

'No hope, I'm sorry. He will have to tell the truth because he will never be able to prove he is someone he is not. A lawyer has spent professional time and effort trying to prove that.'

'So now they could see his position differently.'

'They will see that he has lied.'

'A mistake. A genuine mistake. From ignorance and fear.'

'Mistakes are not forgiven by the Home Office. The system is stacked against any error. People fail for far less. And now Egypt is considered safe again.'

'Can you be sure that he will be safe? He is frightened and with good reason.'

'The Home Office has an arrangement with the government there. If he goes back voluntarily, he will be under that protection.'

'What will happen to him?'

'The best thing is, you go and see if he is outside, and I will give him my advice.'

'Okay, I'll see. He might still be here. He was upset, that's all.'

'You will have to be quick. I still have other people to see.' As Walter rose, Stanley leant forwards and said, 'There can be no mistakes in this system. I promise you, people are refused for small errors, just an inconsistency in their story. But a lie is a lie.'

Walter said, 'Excuse me, sorry,' as he pushed in haste through a group of men who had just arrived and were arguing with the grey-haired woman. She was spreading her hands in a gesture to encourage patience, explaining that they would have to wait and maybe come back next week. He ignored his phone ringing in his pocket. Outside there were only two smokers, one of whom was coughing lavishly over the pavement. There was no sign of Amro. Walter paced back and forwards, searching down the street for any sign of him. Where had he gone? Was he going to miss this chance of assistance?

He came around the corner at the moment Walter had given up and was turning to go back inside.

'I'm here. Sorry. It is hard.'

'Of course, it is, I'm so sorry. But come on, lad. He seems… he is kind, and he knows how to help you.' Walter did not say that he already knew what the help would be, what advice was going to be given.

They went back to sit opposite Stanley at his temporary desk.

'Good. Glad you came back. Now, let me outline the situation. I have rechecked while you were outside so there's no doubt.'

Amro looked at the ground. Walter leant forwards and touched his arm lightly in support.

'You have to accept that you cannot stay here. You are already reporting to the Home Office. You have been detained once – they will detain you soon, and they will deport you. Eventually. It might take months in detention before they get round to you.'

Walter's phone sounded again. There was a text.

'I'm sorry, this is from my daughter. She's pregnant.' He moved away from the desk and read the message.

'Hi, this is Yvette, Gabby's partner. She is in labour. Please come to the hospital.'

He turned to the others, uncertain of what to do.

Amro asked, 'Is it the baby? Then you must go, Walter sir.'

'Yes, I will. But let's hear what Stanley has to say.' He felt he should stay and he should go. He tried to concentrate on this moment here, what was now being said.

'So, to avoid deportation and a possibly long detention, you can accept voluntary repatriation. If you do, the government will support you. You will get a card with money on it to help you get back to your country, to your life there.'

Amro tensed his hands into fists on his lap.

'If you do take this route, you can go home, quite soon. Once a bit more paperwork is done.'

As Amro was silent, Walter asked, 'Who would organise that?'

'I can do that for him. I am happy if he gives me the go-ahead, to start the process now.'

Leaning towards Amro, he spoke gently into his eyes. 'If

you do this, you will be able to come back here, if that is what you really wish. You will be able to apply for asylum again. If you have a case. If things are very bad, if you are a victim of persecution again.'

Amro lifted his eyes and said, 'What if I don't go with this voluntary and they do deport me. I can come back, straight away?'

'If you go as a deportee, your name will be on a list, and it will be ten years before they will consider any application.'

'It is one year or ten? Is that it?' Walter held out his hand to Amro and took hold of his wrist.

'That is the position.'

'And if he paid for another lawyer, to start again with the true story?'

Stanley's expression was wry. His eyes said, who will pay for this?

'No, any lawyer would say the same. In fact, now asylum applications from Egypt have stalled. If he had come this year, he would be refused.'

'Thank you. We will go and discuss it.' Walter moved to rise and nodded to Amro to come.

As they were leaving, Stanley said, 'Come back, Amro, when you are ready, and we will get it started. I can set it up for you. It will be for the best.'

As they came out of the building, pushing through the muddle of people still waiting for advice, Walter saw Amro looked suddenly older. His face had folded into the lines of despair. Walter's helplessness rose up in his chest. He was angry and sad. They stood together on the pavement, saying nothing for several minutes.

'He says you will be safe if you go back,' he said, the words with the query he had turned over so many times but was unspoken so far.

'You have the human rights here. You do not know what it is like when there are no human rights.'

He could find no response to this. Two men pushed past them, one wearing a turban, both agitated and sounding furious in a language he could not identify.

The phone in his hand was insistent. He had been called to go to the hospital.

'It is okay, my friend, I will be alright. Go and I will see you later. Good luck to the baby and the mother.'

'Where will you go?' He held out a hand and, for a second, Amro grasped it. They stood, eyes locked, warm hands clasped, two friends on opposite shores. Amro released his hand and nodded, allowing Walter to go, giving his encouragement.

'I will go to the mosque, my friend. Go and see the new baby, greet the new life which arrives.'

TEN

The hospital entrance hall was enormous, three stories high; an atrium he had learnt to call the design, a lofty space dwarfing the people below. An architect's dream, he supposed. Certainly, it brought light and space, though it also made this place of healing seem like an airport. The information system was hi-tech, with screens everywhere for self-check-in and ward lists. He was too warm in his coat despite the chilly day, as he had walked as quickly as he could from the centre and up through town, past his own street and up the hill to the hospital.

He was glad to see there were also humans ready to help and a volunteer in a yellow tabard showed him where to go for the maternity wards. Here he found a small waiting area with chairs in two rows, a television showing a house search programme and two sad-faced men, one a father-to-be and a grandfather, he thought. Neither acknowledged his arrival.

He sat down, looked around for a magazine or paper to read, but saw only pamphlets about baby food. There was an atmosphere of anxiety and tension in the air which he knew was leaking out from him too. This was a month too early for Gabby's baby. She had been resting on doctor's orders for three weeks as her blood pressure was high.

Out of a door further down the corridor, Yvette appeared and came to shake his hand. They had met once before briefly on a video call when Gabby had shouted to her to come into frame.

'Hi, Walter, so glad you are here.' She was a tall woman, lean and angular, with a springy quality to her body which Walter put down to her work as a PE teacher. She had dark blonde hair, scraped back to show a face as lean as the rest of her. Today she was wearing the kind of soft clothes with a stripe down the sides which he knew were considered chic but he thought of as strictly gym wear. Perhaps she had come from the gym or had left a class session with children in school. It was still the school day. He found her slightly frightening now in person, energetic even in the way she came to sit beside him.

'Is she okay? What is happening?'

'She is doing it. She is bringing that baby into the world, Walter, and she is doing great.' To his embarrassment, she gripped his hand and looked earnestly at him.

'So, everything is going well?' he asked again. 'Didn't she want a home birth?' Gabby had told him all about her birth plan with all the details: the type of soothing music she wanted, the candles, homeopathy remedies on hand, a birthing pool which was still on order, had not been delivered. She had imagined bringing her baby into a world of peace and beauty all around which she had created especially for the baby. Not into this cold, strange place.

'Has something gone wrong?' The question sounded too brutal once it was out.

'It was because it is early, and her blood pressure… the midwife said this was better. She started so fast and now it is going slow! Heyho.' This was an oddly cheerful kind of reflection. 'And it is better to be here, Walter. Me, I never thought it was safe at home.' She was a person of opinions, he thought.

'Is she on her own?'

'Marie is there, her mother, you know,' as if he did not, 'I stepped out to see if you had made it. So glad.' She squeezed his fingers too tightly and then was bounding off back to the far door.

The two men did not look up from their joint study of the ward flooring. The air settled back into expectation and quiet misery.

He remembered the waiting for Celia's birth. He had been in the room with Linda for several hours. It was not compulsory in his day for the man to be at the bedside and witness the event. Many were not. Linda believed it was important for the father to see it all and share the experience, so he had found the decision was made for him. He felt self-conscious at first, as if there was a pattern of behaviour which he had not learnt. The staff in their busy efficiency would realise he had not read the leaflet, "How a man must behave when present at a birth". As the day wore on, he forgot himself. He was glad to be with her, to rub her back and let her grip his hand. He boasted of it afterwards to anyone who would listen. But the birth he remembered as a sequence of colours, hazy flashes with the shock of blood and the blue-veined reality of the baby at last.

Now he was a spare part. Why had he come in such haste? He stood up, restless and uncertain. If he was not needed in the birth room, he would go outside and ring Amro. He spoke to a nurse who was rushing along, reluctant, he saw, to stop for him.

'Gabriella... is she? Is the birth soon? Sorry, I mean, how long do you think it is going to be now?'

'A little while yet,' she told him with that mild tone of pandering to the old which he recognised.

So, he would go outside and make a call. He would breathe in air free of the hospital stink. Yvette would text him if he was needed or anything happened.

In the area immediately outside the circular doors, patients and medics mingled, the staff moving purposefully in one direction or another, the patients aimless or stationary while they used their phones. Two men in wheelchairs, positioned just beyond the sign which said no smoking in this area, were smoking together; one with a leg in plaster, the other with a drip he pushed along. Walter wondered how they had got there and why a passing doctor did not remonstrate.

There was no reply to his first text. He rang the house; no answer. He texted again and asked Amro to contact him straight away. If the boy was in the mosque still, he probably could not use a phone. He rang the house again and left a message.

It was a long afternoon. Walter spent it alternately in front of the hospital, watching the ceaseless coming and going which accelerated in visiting hour, or restlessly sitting in the waiting area. The two men had gone by three o'clock, happy or sad he did not know. A woman joined him for an hour but was whisked away to greet the new life in her family. He realised that there was another area on another corridor and wondered if Gabby was in a ward for difficult births. No one told him anything. Neither Yvette nor Marie appeared. He drank two coffees from the atrium cafe and regretted both. There was no word from Amro.

On one of his trips outside, he saw a couple bringing a baby to their car, the tiny head hidden within the heavy plastic of the car seat which the man carried with conscious pride. Gabby's baby now being brought into life in the room above had no father to carry the heavy things. Would Yvette take the role? Would it be her who taught the need for responsibility and took the boy out for football games? This was an old-fashioned way of thinking, but he could not shake it off on demand. His own father had always been working, always tired from work. He was a painter and decorator who worked shifts at the weekend and evenings to boost the family income. Sunday was the only rest day and was sacred. He and his sister would spend that day with him, sometimes on a family walk, always with a big dinner together, or having to be quiet so his dad could rest and read the paper. He was the respected centre of the family.

Walter had tried to be a more fun father for Celia, ready to roll on the floor, to tease and laugh and cuddle. He taught her the names of birds and flowers on their park walks and waited expectantly for her to be the right age for the first football match. When she grew into teenage years, she began to cling to her mother, to share the world of female secrets. He was not to be included, he understood at length, and football was not going to happen. He had never got her back. Her mother's death had ended that hope in a way he could not fathom.

What did he know about women-to-women sexual relationships? He did not know if they planned for Yvette to be a father figure or even thought in such dimensions. He privately doubted if Gabby was really a lesbian. He would never say such a thing out loud.

His phone pinged in his pocket. At last, Amro. He fumbled for it, so relieved to hear from him that his fingers were unsteady.

"Baby here. All well and safe. Come now".

PART IV

The giant sunflowers have started to collapse in the late September sunshine. Their heavy heads are drooping earthwards on thick stems. He lifts the child up to see the intricate casings which hold hundreds of seeds in each clock face. It is good to breathe in the scent of the boy's head. But Harry leans back in protest, his face screwed up with concentration. He wriggles and kicks his legs so fiercely that one red plastic boot falls to the ground. Walter laughs and releases him. He wants to be down and to wobble off again along the bumpy path. Walter follows him, boot in hand, catching at him to make him stop long enough to put the boot back on. Harry grudgingly agrees to pause for a moment.

'He is never still,' his mother grimaces lovingly. 'Never for a minute until he falls asleep. And then he is restless all night, throwing the duvet off. I have to go and smooth it over. Sometimes he is crushed right up against the corner of the cot. We can't put him in a bed. He would just fall out.'

'It's because he is so healthy. It's marvellous, really marvellous when you think how he started.'

She runs up after the little boy, holding out her hand for him to hold so she can steer him away from the brambles now stretching out over the path. He consents to be led. The blackberries are over, soft now without sweetness, but he saved the last ones in the freezer, and they are snug in the pie baked ready for supper. Their picnic is waiting for Celia to arrive. He clears the pot of carrot sticks, tiny squares of brown sandwiches half sucked and the jar of savoury puree off the bench, the remains of Harry's feast. Cheese scones and a tomato salad, made with the rich glory of his last harvest, are ready for the adults, packed away in his basket with a flask of homemade lemonade. He sits with a bump, grateful for the rest. It has been a long, warm morning with the boy's fizz of energy sapping his own.

Gabriella and Harry make their wandering way along the edge of the other plots, stopping to study every beanpole, every bee and to attempt to catch the dance of every cabbage butterfly weaving past. When they reach the apple trees, where globes of apples red and green lie half hidden on the grass, he escapes his mother's restricting hand to run among the windfalls, picking up half-eaten or mouldy ones. Gabby is in close pursuit to ease each one out of his fingers.

Watching them from the bench, Walter thinks back to those early days of the boy's life, when they could only see him through the plastic of a hospital cot. He had been allowed to visit as he had been given the privilege and honour of being a named family member. The room was quiet, darkened, with another sick baby also being tended by the nurse. He was uncertain how to behave as he stared at this tiny body. He felt fear and dread each time he crossed the corridor to enter. Slowly he became accustomed to the sight of this beginning of a life. He was able to make the right kind of noises, say suitable things to Gabby as she held the baby's hand through an aperture.

Now the boy is a robust toddler, no sign of that bad early start in his chubby, ever stronger legs. His pompous name, Harrison, has become a warm shorthand. Walter has lost any association with loud fellow gardener Harry on the plot – this is the only Harry he knows now.

He was one year old this week, a birthday marked with much ceremony by Yvette and Gabriella. Walter found the party overwhelmingly noisy: adults in clusters ignoring their children, drink in hand; babies running or crying, extravagant with piles of gifts enough for several children. But he was the guest of honour as the named grandfather. So, he enjoyed that at least.

Gabriella has risen to the challenge of motherhood. She is still on maternity leave, extended because of the premature birth. She has negotiated an imminent return to work on a part-time basis. She and Yvette enjoy the child; it is so clear to anyone who sees them. He wonders at their confidence and practical attitude to all the inevitable complications. He sees Yvette rarely but hears about her a great deal – whenever Gabby comes to visit, at least once a fortnight, she talks. She tells him how they share bath time when Yvette comes home from school, how the night-time feeding was on a rota from the first. 'Yvette is his mother too,' she asserts to Walter's continuing confusion.

They are coming back now, Harry charging ahead, his feet going faster and faster on the slope so that Gabby has to run to catch him and Walter is on his feet ready to save him a tumble at the gate. As she swoops him up in her arms, making him giggle with a tickle on his tummy, Celia's car appears outside. He goes to help her disembark. She is intent on the struggle of lifting the child seat out of the back, plus the large holdall necessary for all her accessories. These are not necessities in Walter's view. Every possible additional baby object and gadget has been added to Celia's small flat, crowding the floor and the little shelf space available. Much of it has to be brought with her, turning every visit into an expedition.

'Let me help you, love.' He takes the holdall. Gabby is waiting near the gate to greet her, Harry now clinging to her legs, suddenly overcome by the arrival of new people. Celia carries the seat up to the bench, hardly looking up until she has deposited it safely on the grass.

'Hello to lovely Lily.' He stretches out his arms to take the child. But her mother intervenes.

'She's fine there for now. She's sleepy from the journey, Dad.'

He bends over his grandchild, this perfect creature with her pearly skin and strands of the finest fair hair. This is the baby Linda might have been.

'Hello, Harry.' Celia tries to get the boy to come towards her, but he resists, turning his head determinedly away. 'Oh well. Playing hard to get. How are you, Gabby?'

'Fine. We've had such a lovely time, haven't we, Harry? Tell Auntie Celia what we have been doing with Gramps.'

She lifts up the toy spade and trowel he had bought for him which, in fact, have been unused today and the other days; they are far less interesting to the child's eye than the buzzing expanse of the gardens all around.

'Of course. My dad is so good with children, especially babies.'

Celia leans down to lift Lily out of the seat and give her now to Walter. He takes the weight of the baby against his chest, smiling over her head at the two women. Linda would have laughed at Celia's witness – he had struggled to be confident holding Celia as a baby; he was always ready to pass her back to her waiting mother whose hands were always outstretched. He feels lucky to hold lovely Lily. She opens sleepy eyes and gazes with a startled concentration at him.

Celia sits beside him, and they both stare at the baby. Motherhood has softened Celia's outline, after an anxious pregnancy when she seemed to get thinner as her belly swelled. She is rounder. Today she leans towards Walter for a second, a swift pressure on his shoulder.

*

Alone in the middle of the city, above the streets and the life of other people, other families, discharged from the hospital after only two days, Celia rang her father. He drove there immediately. He found her sunk in a muddle of sleeplessness and panic. The elation and joy of the birth, with Art and Walter both celebrating at her side, had washed away in a desperate tide of loneliness and pain. He knew Gabby had

had her mother sleeping at their house for many days before Harry was settled and strong. Walter wondered if he could manage this himself. Where was Linda who would take charge, know how to react, know what to say?

'Go back to bed, love,' he instructed firmly. 'I will feed her; I'll be fine. Go on.' He found he remembered how to hold the tiny body upright and close so she relaxed. He could tilt the bottle correctly after a few minutes. Linda had breast fed their daughter, so he had never learnt this skill, but he knew this was a simple procedure as long as he stayed calm. He took the baby out for a walk, managing to get down in the lift with the enormous pushchair contraption that apparently was the latest thing, walking the urban streets with a certain lift to his head. When he made it back to the flat with a sleeping Lily, Celia was washed and looked better. 'Dad. Please, can you stay the night.' She offered him her bed in a desperate appeal. It would be hard to leave her.

He stayed, piling a duvet onto Celia's white couch, the cushions slipping off as he turned over in another fruitless attempt to find comfort. His feet brushed the end, so he had to curl into a Z shape to doze at all. He heard the baby's cries and, half-awake, managed one of the three feeds that night, soothing the child with a little nursery rhyme refrain which came unbidden to his tongue. By early morning he had straightened his legs with an effort and was downstairs making tea and toast for them both. He was stiff and exhausted. He hugged her as his good morning and she leant into him, soft and accepting.

At lunchtime, Art and Rich rang the bell, arms full of more flowers, gift-wrapped baby clothes and fluffy bunnies with big eyes. The flat shrunk with their arrival, tall, energetic, smiling men entering a space transformed by milky odours, damp cloths, disorder and lack of sleep. Walter offered them soup and stayed downstairs while they sat with Celia and cooed over the baby. He could hear them talking on the mezzanine. There was no privacy provided in this layout.

'Why don't you come and stay with us? We have lots of space; you can have your own room; we are both out at work usually, but I have paternity leave to come so I can take it when you like.'

'We will look after you.' This was Rich.

Walter made more tea. The stairs were surprisingly steep with a tray in hand. He put it down carefully on the small table.

'Celia, you can come to me. Come home, love, for a while. That would be best.'

Both men looked up, startled at his interruption. The word paternity was swirling in Walter's head. This man was the biological father then – he had not been very sure until now. Celia's eyes filled with tears. She shook her head.

'Thanks, Dad. But I can't. All this stuff,' she gestured around at baby blankets, feeding mat, basket, stuff, 'and the midwife. And…' She tailed off.

'All this can go in the car. We'll manage no problem.' He was certain now she must come. Art, the father, was quiet, watching, saying nothing. Walter thought he was going to object.

'I can arrange for you to have a midwife at home. I can speak to your GP and get that organised for you.' He saw Rich was supporting him now. He nodded authoritatively at him, yes this would work, this was for the best. 'Art and Rich can visit you at home, at my house, isn't that right? You will be very welcome whenever it suits you.'

So, they packed the car high, with Celia squashed in the back and the baby in her chair filling the front seat. He drove so slowly that day, taking the motorway as if it was a quiet country lane where they were enjoying the scenery, mindful of a precious cargo. Lorries hooted at him as they passed in disgust.

Lily was healthy, but she cried unceasingly in those first few nights and days, a protest into the world. The midwife's reassurance about her weight failed to convince Celia, so accustomed to control, that all was well. Slowly the baby calmed; slowly her mother began to accept and to take charge. Walter held his granddaughter, breathed in the scent of her new skin and felt his heart fill.

For a fortnight, mother and child filled his life, but now they are back in the flat, the motorway to Manchester, the struggle to park somewhere not too expensive, the walk along city streets to her block, the lift up to her flat, these have become part of his week. He prepares meals to take and leave for her to eat when he has gone. He picks her the first strawberries, searching under the leaves for the best and ripest. He stews soup from his lettuces and early peas, tasting carefully to make sure he is not using too much salt.

It is still hard to leave her each time. His daughter's face is less strained though, her confidence handling the baby greater. She greets him as he arrives with relief and also a new warmth that he can store and take home with him. After each visit, feeling tired in his legs and his heart, he has to give himself a day of inactivity. The allotment must wait until his energy rises again.

The contract she has drawn up with Art and his partner Rich stipulates that the couple will have Lily for a weekend twice a month. But in those early days, Celia could only release the baby out of her arms to her father, and only for a short walk or one feed. Tired, overanxious, unsure of herself and uneasy about every possible wrong thing she might do, she was unable to accept the baby leaving her side to go somewhere else.

Together, she and Walter agreed that the contract with the two men was for the long term. Art is a reasonable, kind man, perhaps as unused to children as Celia herself. He agreed to come and see them at the flat and share Lily that way at first. One lucky thing Walter can acknowledge is that his partner, Rich, is a source for them of calm, knowledgeable advice. A voice to consult about every skin rash, every change in feeding pattern, every approach to how to establish sleep.

*

Today they are to have a picnic, the two women, the two children, on his patch, the sun giving them this day of real warmth, when the colours of the season are changing to golden and red and the harvests are still plentiful. The air is full of the aromas of fruitfulness. Walter spreads out his offerings on a blanket. Harry has to be coaxed to sit for a little while on his mother's lap and suck a bottle. Lily goes back to sleep in the shade. Gabby and Celia relax over crumbs of scone and chilled lemonade from his flask.

'Dad, how's your refugee? Have you heard from him?'

'He did go back, didn't he? Is he okay?'

'Remind us, how did it happen?'

Walter turns to them and begins to relate the tale as he has tried before. He is not sure these two young women, wrapped up in their immediate lives, generous in their own ways, kind as he would wish them to be, have ever understood what happened or why or how he feels about it, but he is clear that such a story needs to be remembered. He will always remember it and will always wonder if he could have done something more, something to change the outcome.

'Stanley, the advisor at the Sanctuary Centre, organised it with the Home Office. There was some paper stuff, lots of phone calls. Amro went down there every week for a bit to see him, get it sorted.'

'So, he accepted it. Was he happy to go, in the end I mean, going home to his family after such a horrible time here?' Gabby strokes Harry's head as she says this, and the little boy closes his eyes.

'He had no choice. He was very upset at first.' Helpless rage had filled his own days after the advice was given, while Amro had gone inside himself, hardly speaking and with empty eyes. Walter lay awake wondering how else he could help, what the route could be, so that the young man's path would not go in this direction, backwards. He tried to find out if Amro would be in danger in Egypt. He read journalists' reports of what had happened to the street protesters at first and what might happen now. There was no reassurance to be found, no safe place in that information. He saw that the death penalty was being used to stifle dissent.

'He was very strong. He stayed very quiet for a few days. He hardly spoke. But then he decided. He had to go and make the best of it. He would see his family at least. His mother, he had not seen her for so long.' He thinks of the darkness in Amro's face lightening when he spoke of seeing his parents, and especially his mother, again.

'Did you persuade him?' Celia smiles at him. 'You didn't want him to go, did you? But you accepted it, you knew it was right.'

He wants to shout into the soft, early autumn air, 'I knew it was wrong.'

'Ironic that if he had told the truth in the first place, he wouldn't have been in that position.'

Walter does not comment. They cannot understand how one mistake can betray the future, how the system turns people into grains under the wheel.

'So, at last it was all put together and he left, a year nearly it is now. He went down to London to get the flight with an escort. Oh yes, they were not going to let him out of their sight at that stage.'

'And he had money to go back with, didn't he? An allowance so he would not be destitute like he was here. That must have been a real help.' Celia sounds pleased, ignoring, or not hearing, the tone of his voice as he remembers.

'You were a good friend to him, Pops. He must have been very grateful.'

'He wrote to me, left a letter in his room. A farewell and thank you.'

'That's good. I bet you were delighted to get that.' Celia goes over to the pushchair and checks on Lily.

He cannot tell them how he had held the letter in his hand for hours before reading it. He walked down to his patch and read it at last as the evening light softened the outlines of trees and hedges and cast a fading glow on the lines of seedlings. Amro's written English was not as good as his spoken, but each sentence was a tiny blow to the heart. The paper was still folded into Walter's diary.

He does not tell them how he and Amro had sat together in the last evening. He made tea and they sat as the liquid cooled, with little it was possible to say. At one point, Amro got to his feet in one fluid, urgent move and went out of the house. Walter waited and an hour later he came back in, pale but composed, his face now with its new lines and his eyes clouded. Walter made another pot of tea and then cut bread for sandwiches. Amro shook his head but accepted toast later, thick with butter and last year's jam. When his guest had gone upstairs to bed for the last time, Walter found he could not follow him. He could not sit and let his feet settle back into stillness. He walked around the house, picking up newspapers, putting kitchen objects in order, cleaning surfaces, planning the breakfast he would make. He picked up the new hardback copy of *Tess of the d'Urbervilles* he had bought to put in Amro's bag, a little memory for him to take on the journey back.

He waited for the dreaded morning to come. The door to Amro's room stayed closed and he was silent. Sleep came only in the early hours.

He cannot share with the two mothers how he had felt the emptiness of the house in the days after Amro's departure. How restless he had been. How he had felt sadness drag him downwards so that the pattern of life was invisible to him.

How he could not find belonging even on his allotment where he looked up to see a stranger's outline and found none. How he had struggled to find himself in his place again. Linda's wraith had deserted him; he could not see her on his plot, where there were few green shoots in a slow spring.

'So, he is safe, yes, he got home and nothing bad happened to him?'

'There was a real problem with the money actually. It was supposed to be linked to this card they gave him, a kind of cash card. But it didn't work.'

'What did he do?'

'Well. We spent hours on the phone to the Home Office.'

'You, we? Spent hours?'

'Stanley and the others at the Sanctuary Centre. I went down and helped out and we tried and tried to get through. They kept promising it would be there. It was weeks before he had any cash at all.'

'But he managed, yes? He has family there after all.' Walter thinks of the photos Amro has sent of his family's small concrete house, his father and mother, frail and uncertain in front of the camera.

'And he wasn't picked up when he got home, the police there haven't taken him?' He knows how fearful Amro was in the last few days before he had to go. He was terrified, despite Stanley's repeated assurances, that there might be a welcome committee of armed police at the airport.

'The Home Office assured him that they have an agreement with the government there, that he would be safe.'

'So, your refugee saga is over, Pops. You did what you could, and all is well.'

'You are going down now as a volunteer to the Centre, aren't you?' The truth was that the time he spent at the Sanctuary Centre filled part of the week, the days; it answered some of the wondering too. It eased his heart to offer friendship, to give support. He could not admit to these young women that he did not do it for those others. He did it for himself. He feels he is now someone who can help, who knows enough to do so. He is pleased to be known as someone who can be relied on, who is now part of the movement to defeat and subvert the system. The sky has lifted for him. He can see further than before.

'You are going to carry on. That's great. If it suits you, Dad. Well done you.'

They are both satisfied. They have abandoned the subject. It is time to go, for the two mothers to take their children back to his house, Celia to stay for a couple of days, Gabby to have a cup of tea before she goes home to Yvette. The packing up takes a few moments, the picnic cleared away, the remains put carefully back into his basket, the baby and toddler lifted into the cars. He sets off to walk back around the corner while they are sorting out all the paraphernalia of modern childhood. As he nears the end of his own street, Sue passes him in a car, hooting her horn in greeting as she goes past. He lifts a rueful arm in reply. Now he is a grandfather first and foremost, for everyone to see. How foolish he has been to think anyone would see him differently, he muses as he comes home and puts the kettle on. He is pleased now that he did not try to persuade Sue to see him as a man, a potential mate, a bedfellow. He has kept his dignity and she has been spared that embarrassment. She is a friend, and he can be grateful for that. Old age is a fool and does not know it.

He once hoped for Gabby and Celia to bond over the project of child raising, both women of a similar age, without a proper father for the child, both with professional work to return to – he had dreamed of a new cosiness between them, shared outings, long exchanges of information, even a regular pattern of travel between the city and Manchester. Now he is grateful to have them as it is, to have them both near him, for it to be possible to be together with them as today. These two new lives have brought him joy; they have renewed his energy for life. They came and love came too. Love is not a cake to be sliced, partitioned out. He can put his arms around them all. He can keep the women and the children safe. Celia will see how his love for the precious granddaughter is not reduced by his love for little Harry.

Later that day, as Celia is feeding Lily upstairs in the dusk of evening, he walks back to the allotment to do more watering. He had to stop this morning. Harry so delighted in catching the rainbow spray that the little boy was quickly in danger of becoming sodden and Walter gave up.

The evening light is fading; the days are closing in. A breeze is curling around the shed and bending seed heads. He walks his patch, hardly noticing the crops he can still gather, the ones which have collapsed and will be no good. His head and heart are full of the tale of Amro. He did not tell the women how at first he had messages every week, how he and Amro passed photos, texts, queries to each other. He wrote them all down in his notebook. Now, this evening, he cannot shake off his anxiety for him; there has been no word from him for a fortnight, no response to Walter's queries. He learns from some of the texts that Amro is unhappy back in his own country, though he does not know exactly why. Amro says "It is bad here". The fear that now something has happened to the young man preoccupies him, lingers into the evenings and the dawns. With dread, he reads reports of the current situation in Egypt. He sees that Amnesty is collating details of arbitrary arrests, prisoners maltreated, executions.

He tries to remember that Amro may have lost interest in his old English friend. He is young after all. He will be busy making his new life, the time as an asylum seeker in England part of the past. He has said his thank yous. It is enough.

As he comes up to the fruit trees, there is the fox, an old man fox dragging his thick tail a little closer to the ground now, walking along the edge of the orchard by the lowered branches of the plum. In his pocket the phone goes. With great relief he sees it is a message from Amro.

"I am going to Kaliningrad to cross to Germany. Egypt very bad position".

Walter messages back "Let me know how you are, where you are". He wonders where Kaliningrad is and why it is a destination. He will look it up at home. Amro is leaving again, will be a refugee seeking asylum again. How little he knows of this man's life; his friend will be a lost traveller again, going somewhere on the road but never arriving.

The fox has stopped on its pathway. The creature looks across the grass, through the trees, at Walter. He salutes him silently. The fox belongs here as much as he does.

It is dark as he goes back to the house. He comes into a peaceful kitchen, where Celia is relieved that baby Lily is finally asleep. He offers her hot chocolate. As he heats enough milk for two, the phone goes again. He will look at it later on his own. Now he sits with his daughter, talking quietly over the day.

'Your mother would be so proud of you,' he says to her softly as she leaves the room. She turns to smile. He no longer looks for Linda these days. He sees her in the lines of his daughter's face as she bends over her baby.

When he is on his way to bed, he reads the message: "If I succeed, it will be hard way. Love to you and to your family all". Walter sits on the edge of the bed and reads the message again. He puts the phone aside and lies down to sleep, full of worry about what the hard way might mean for Amro. He sleeps fitfully, until the baby wakes him in the dark hours with her reedy cry for food. He hears Celia hushing her with soothing words and a little comfort song. His daughter is being a mother. How joyful Linda would have been to hear her.

In the morning, he reads the words on his phone again and begins to wait for another message. His own new happiness is always marked by this dark question: could I have done more for him? Where is he now?

*

There is always another message. Sometimes there is a gap of months, but always there is another. When the text flashes and he sees a strange number, he knows it will be Amro. He is in yet another place, sometimes he does not say where. Much later, when another year has turned, he stays put. He is in Germany. He is learning German. One day he mentions a woman; her name is Sofia. He sends a photo of a serious looking girl with dark eyes and straight, fair hair. Walter smiles to think of the handsome man using his charms again, to be liked, to be safe and cared for again. He chooses to believe that the journey has now come to an end. He thinks perhaps Amro has arrived.

He wrote the date and time and the wording of that first message, saying Amro was leaving Egypt, in his notebook for that year. It is still his habit to keep the notebook for one year into the next, using Spring as the beginning, following the annual turn of the seasons and the harvests in his garden and noting any small thoughts or observations he had; how many times he saw the fox, for instance, or the temperature and date. He had included a note of the times that he had seen Amro, or Osama as he was then. Later, a note about which dish had been a success with his housemate.

In that way, he can always look back and see how and when he planted and how successful each effort was. Or how unsuccessful. Then he will put that notebook aside and look at it only to compare the types of seed or variety of potato, to remind himself when was a good time to plant and when it was too early, risking the decimation of seedlings by frost. He always chooses the same type of notebook, metal ring bound so that it will open flat and usually a blue one as the colour of hope and sky. A new notebook means clean, blank pages and another year to plan and hope for. An old one lasts for much of the next year for reference, before he can decide to throw it away.

He begins the habit of putting down the messages from Amro. The texts are on his phone. But he likes to see them as words, the dates forming a line down the page. He keeps a section at the back for this special record. He likes to think it is there. Now he has made space for the notebooks to be stacked into the bookcase – he does not throw any away.

The notebooks for the year of Amro, from when he came into Walter's life until he left, stay on his bedside cabinet and are there all through the years to come until the end.